Inevitable Consequences

The Bayou Sisters
BOOK 3

D1529028

Tess

Flowers

Copyright ©2023 Tess Flowers

All rights reserved. This book contains material protected under International and Federal Copyright Laws and Treaties. Any unauthorized reprint or use of this material is prohibited. No part of this book may be reproduced or transmitted in any form or by any means, electronic or mechanical, including photocopying, recording, or any information storage and retrieval system without express written permission from the author/publisher.

This is a work of fiction. Any references or similarities to actual events, real people, living or dead, or to the real locals are intended to give the novel a sense of reality. Any similarity in other names, characters, places, and incidents are entirely coincidental.

GRAB YOUR FREE COPY OF "WHERE IT ALL BEGUN"

www.authortessflowers.com/sample

This book is dedicated to my sisters, Szilvia and Adrienne, my nephew, Leo, my father, and in loving memory of my mother.

TABLE OF CONTENTS

PROLOGUE

Alexis sat paralyzed, staring at the glossy black coffin. Were it not for the tears clouding her vision, she'd be able to see her reflection. Inside the eternal tomb was her father—her world, gone forever. Her youngest sister clenched her hand tightly, distracting Alexis from the hole in her heart.

The voices in her head drowned out the sobbing and painful cries that surrounded her. Alexis's labored breathing made her body feel heavy and numb at the same time.

Glancing down, she watched her sister's hand slowly slide away. Alexis's gaze rose to meet Mackenzie's. Her lips were moving, but no sound came out as she mouthed something over and over. Squinting her eyes, Alexis tried to make out what she was saying, and when she couldn't figure it out, she told her, "I can't hear you."

Mackenzie's lips continued to move, but every sound was muffled. Then, as if someone

1

turned up the volume, she heard Mackenzie say, "They're laughing at you!"

She repeated it several times before Alexis tuned in to what she was saying.

"Why are they laughing at you? Lexi… look," she said, pointing behind them.

As Alexis turned her head, the cackling grew louder. She stared confusedly at the people before turning around to find Grace and Rose laughing hysterically.

"She doesn't even know," Grace mocked.

Rose added, "He's not even her father. What is she crying for?"

Leslie stood with her arms crossed, shaking her head in disbelief.

Alexis recognized the contemptuous gaze. It was the same one Leslie gave her and Mackenzie when they found themselves in trouble with their parents.

Beside Leslie was their grief-stricken mother. Alexis searched her eyes for empathy, or maybe pity—some kind of an indication that she *wasn't alone, but it was as if she was looking straight through her. Alexis studied her family and the room at large until her eyes landed on a tall, blurry silhouette standing next to Grace. She couldn't make out who it was, but she saw the mysterious figure was pointing and laughing too.*

"Lexi...Lexi, what are they talking about?" Mackenzie asked over and over.

Their voices elevated as the cackling and whispering pierced her eardrums.

"Secret baby..."

"Outcast..."

"Who's her real father?"

"Does she even know?"

It was just one insult after the next. The taunting was relentless.

"You're never going to find out... you're never going to find out... you're nev— "

CHAPTER ONE

Five days ago….
FRIDAY, 3 A.M.

"No… no…no!" Alexis jolted out of her sleep, sitting straight up, fighting to breathe.

The fan blades echoed around the room as she tried to gain control of her erratic breathing and thumping heart as a thick layer of perspiration covered her skin. The waves of cool air from above chilled the sweat beads rolling down her chest and back.

Alexis placed her hand over her heart just as the hand of another touched the small of her back. She briefly closed her eyes as the gradual massages glided over her back, moving the moisture from one side to the other. She remembered where she was now. Once her heart rate steadied, she peeked over her shoulder, and her eyes met his. They were comforting, unlike her mother's look in her dream.

Feeling her pulse underneath his palm, Keith gazed at her curiously. "Are you okay?" he asked, voice groggy.

He assumed she'd had a bad dream, especially since he could have sworn, he heard her muttering in her sleep throughout the night. Keith didn't know what the nightmares were about, but Alexis seemed rattled.

Though the frazzled look in her eyes hadn't disappeared, her breathing slowed. He hadn't expected her to arrive at his door last night, but he wasn't complaining either. She showed up unannounced with two bottles of bourbon. They drank a bottle then she barely said two words before ripping his clothes off.

Any chance he got to hold her; he'd take it. Whenever she let her guard down, he found her to be her most beautiful, but her passion was like kryptonite. He loved how she felt pressed up against him. Warm. Soft. Perfect, even. Still, the analytical side of him couldn't help but wonder what led her to his door.

They had done this back-and-forth for close to a year and a half; most times, it usually ended with her saying she couldn't do this anymore and telling him it was the last time. Other times she'd just show up, they'd have sex, and she'd be gone by morning, leaving him to try to figure out just what was going on between them.

But that was typical of Alexis.

Minimum conversation smothered beneath alcohol and passion. Keith assumed it was how she coped with her obvious commitment issues. He didn't mind being physical, but he wanted to be more than her stress relief, her drinking buddy, or her occasional booty call when she needed an itch scratched. He honestly had more to offer her than this. Keith rested his palm on his forehead as he continued to study her.

He tried to recall what she said last night, yet some of the details were fuzzy. He did, however, remember her saying, "They lied to me," repeatedly. She never revealed who "they" were. He'd learned a while ago to just let her talk when she was in a zone; otherwise, she'd shut down completely.

Despite her relationship stance, he appreciated that she felt he was a safe place to run. Some people might say she was using him— keeping him on a shelf until she was ready to entertain him—but he didn't see it that way. Unlike most people, Keith saw a side of Alexis that he knew she didn't reveal often.

Leaning forward, he gently placed a kiss on her lower back. Alexis flinched when his lips connected with her skin. Her reaction didn't bother him since he knew resistance was second nature to her. Regardless of how much she pretended she didn't have feelings for him, he knew she did. And he wasn't ready to give up on her. Her rebellious nature was just one of the things that attracted him to her.

"Mmm," she groaned.

Keith grinned. Even in the middle of the night, without an ounce of makeup, she was still beautiful. Her skin was perfectly tanned thanks to the Louisiana sun she'd been in for the past two weeks. Her long hair was constrained at the top of her head in a messy bun.

"Bad dream?" he asked.

Still glancing over her shoulder at him, she said, "Something like that."

Even though he knew there was a strong possibility she'd say no, he felt compelled to ask, "Do you want to talk about it?"

"Do I ever?" she replied.

Alexis' thoughts raced. Her dream had felt so real. All of the people, her sisters, her mother, and everyone in attendance, were laughing at her being the only person who didn't know her family's coveted secret. Alexis rubbed her temple as she tried to remember who the blurry face was standing next to Grace, but she couldn't.

She couldn't even make out the deep, baritone voice that drowned out everyone else. He was a stranger to her. A figment of her imagination. A secret that, if left up to Grace, she'd never uncover.

Grace, she thought. She was still trying to wrap her brain around her sister being her mother. She suddenly felt like one of those people on talk shows who didn't know who they belonged to. Her own family had betrayed her.

"Lexi," Keith called, snapping her out of her thoughts.

Alexis exhaled a frustrated breath.

"We don't have to talk about it if you don't want to."

"Honestly, I don't even know where to start, Keith. It's like I've been living a lie my whole life. You know we always tell our patients' families how things can change in the blink of an eye, but I never really thought about how that could apply to me, too."

Keith furrowed his brow. "What do you mean?"

He wasn't sure what had occurred between the time he'd last seen her and her showing up at his front door.

"I mean, my whole life, I've been living under the same roof with people who'd been lying to me like it was nothing." She shook her head. "Now I get it. Now I understand why I would periodically get these awkward looks from Grace, Leslie, and our mother—well, my grandmother... It all makes sense now."

Her grandmother? Keith thought? *What was she talking about?* "What makes sense, Lexi?"

"I'm the family secret," she mumbled.

Keith tried to piece it together but couldn't make heads or tails of it. He didn't know her family that well, but from the few conversations they had about them, they seemed close. He gripped her sides and pulled her toward him. She leaned back as he held her, nestling against his chest while laying on her side.

Tears escaped her eyes, and she wiped them away. This wasn't what she came here for, but after fleeing her parents' house so abruptly, she didn't want to be alone. Thanks to the unsettling nightmare, the alcohol she'd drowned her sorrows in had run its course. Now she was left to deal with her feelings, and the only person she cared to talk to was no longer here.

She was angry at everyone, including her father, but she desperately wanted to talk to him one last time. She wanted to know why he had never thought to tell her the truth. Why, now, did he finally push Grace to say something? Why hadn't he revealed the truth himself? Why was it necessary to lie to her all these years?

Keith tightened his grip around her. And for whatever reason, it was the most comforting thing she felt. She squeezed her eyelids to prevent any more tears from falling. Slow, stagnant breaths flowed from her lips as thoughts bombarded her left and right. From what she gathered, everyone knew she was Grace's daughter except her and Mackenzie.

On the drive to Keith's, when her mind replayed the altercation between Leslie and Grace at the estate, she realized Leslie had also known. It was why Grace had gotten so defensive when Leslie called her deadbeat mother.

"I'm here to listen," Keith said softly, once again pulling her out of her thoughts.

Alexis rolled over to face him. Keith peered into her glassy brown eyes. His heart dropped at the sight of her crying. He'd never seen this side of Alexis before. Aggressive, yes. Sassy, definitely. Occasionally even funny, but never sad.

"I don't even know how to say this, so I'm just going to say it…I recently found out that my parents aren't *actually* my parents. Apparently, my oldest sister, Grace got pregnant when she was a teenager, and to keep things under wraps, they adopted me."

Keith's eyes widened, but he didn't say a word. This seemed like the perfect time to ask questions, but he figured there was more to the story.

"And to make matters worse, everyone knew but me. Well, not everyone. It seems me and

Mackenzie were kept in the dark," she uttered with contempt.

There were a million scenarios he could've come up with in his head, but this wouldn't have been one of them. This was along the lines of Jerry Springer, maybe even a daytime soap opera drama. He searched his mind for the right words to say and came up empty. What did a person say at a time like this?

"Lexi…I-I—" he started to say but stopped.

"You don't have to say anything. I know it's messed up. Hell, I don't even know what to say."

"What did your mother—I mean your—I'm not sure what to call her," he said, realizing he was confused.

Alexis snickered derisively. She didn't either, if she were being honest. Her mother was her grandmother, her sister was her mother, and her other sisters were her aunts. Then there was the question of her paternity.

"She's been my mother my entire life, so calling her that isn't wrong," she told him.

"Besides, I have no intention of ever calling Grace mother."

The snide way she said that didn't escape Keith. However, he felt the hurt it carried. Whenever she talked about her sisters before, she spoke of Grace with the most admiration. It wasn't odd seeing she was the younger sister, and she looked up to her, but what fell from her lips at this moment was worlds away from that.

"I understand. What did your mother say?"

"Nothing of relevance. Like Grace, she gave me the runaround."

A puzzled look formed on his face. "I don't understand. Then how did you find out?"

"I overheard Grace and my mother talking. Apparently, our father gave Grace a letter regarding me and her. She and our mother discussed it when I was heading back to the front of the house. It was merely coincidental that I found out."

"I see," was all he could say since every time she gave more of the story, it worsened. "So, you overheard them, then what?"

"We got into this huge argument because I started asking questions, and no one would answer them."

"Such as?"

"Like, who's my *real* father, for instance. And why no one said anything to me about this after all this time, but I got nothing. No explanations, not even an apology for lying to me about my entire existence."

Alexis felt herself getting angry all over again.

"Wow," Keith said, trying to process everything.

"Exactly."

Rolling onto her back, Alexis stared at the ceiling. She'd never felt more alone than she did now. This was exactly why she didn't let people in. Whenever she let her guard down, people found a way to disappoint her.

"What are you going to do?"

She shrugged. "Honestly, I don't know. When I asked both my mother and my older sisters who my father was, they closed ranks."

"Do you think there was foul play involved?"

Alexis clenched her hand around the sheet she had pulled up over her breasts. The thought had crossed her mind as she drove like a madwoman to get to his place. It would make sense. The secrets…the lies…the cover story. It would also explain why Grace hated being home for longer than a few days, but she ruled it out the minute they all refused to tell her who he was. No way would they protect a predator…unless something bad happened, and that's why she didn't want to rehash those feelings or that experience.

"I don't know what to think, Keith. I won't lie and say the thought didn't cross my mind, but if that were the case, why wouldn't she just say that?"

"Well, for starters, that's not an easy thing to talk about. You and I both know that from the plethora of rape victims—adults and children that come into the hospital."

She nodded knowingly. "You're right," she agreed, "But honestly, I don't think that's what happened."

"Then what?"

Alexis turned her head to face him. "I can't help but wonder if he was somebody older or married who she got wrapped up with, and to save her precious reputation. They swept it under the rug."

"Wouldn't that be the same as your original thought?" Keith inquired.

Alexis scoffed. "Not exactly, at least not in those days. It's not an uncommon thing for an older man to approach younger girls. Though as protective as my father was, I'm beginning to doubt that's what happened. That only leaves someone they didn't approve of. I don't know. Maybe he was a troublemaker or something."

Keith didn't argue with her even though it was all the same in his book. An older man preying on a young girl was not okay. But he knew firsthand the age difference in those days was not enforced as severely as they are now. He remembered going to school with girls who had older boyfriends.

"You don't need them to tell you who he is; you know that right?"

"What do you mean?"

"I mean, you can search the county records. Birth certificates are public records, so all you need to do is get a copy of your birth certificate."

He's right, she thought. She didn't know if it would work, but she didn't have many options, especially since no one wanted to tell her who he was. She was going to have to figure it out on her own.

CHAPTER TWO

"Mackenzie Rae Bayou or whatever your name is...wake up!" Rose shouted. "Get up, Mickey!" Rose shook her leg roughly.

Mackenzie whined as she turned over, pulling the cover over her head.

Rose slapped her thigh this time. "Mickey, get up!"

Flinging the covers back, Mackenzie yelled, "What, Rose?" annoyed that her sister was disturbing her sleep. "Why are you waking me up?"

She had a rough night, thanks to the nausea, and all she wanted to do was sleep. Her morning sickness—that stuck around all day—was killing her. Not to mention, whenever she closed her eyes, she heard Nina's scream and Jasper's voice echoing in her mind.

21

"Get up! Gigi and I need to have a conversation with you."

Mackenzie groaned loudly. "About what?"

"Get up and see," Rose said before turning to walk out.

She and Grace had been stewing all night over what the sheriff had told them. Grace wanted to confront her last night, but after everything that had occurred with Lexi, Rose thought it'd be better if they waited until today.

One family crisis at a time.

"Is she up?" Grace asked as she rounded the corner and walked into the kitchen.

"Not willingly, but yeah, she's up."

Rose accepted the coffee Grace handed her. The warm steam brushed against the tip of her nose as the caffeinated aroma drifted up her nostrils. To be honest, she felt she needed something a lot stronger than coffee to have this conversation, but since it wasn't even noon yet, she'd save the hard stuff for later. Knowing her sisters, she'd need it.

"And you're sure you don't want Mama to be here for this?" Rose asked Grace.

Grace shook her head. "No, Mama has a lot going on right now. The last thing she needs to hear is that her youngest child is on the run from her husband, who no one knew existed, on top of being a "missing person." Let's see what's going on first before we loop her in."

Rose nodded in agreement even though she felt they should tell their mother. After yesterday, the last thing she wanted was for another secret to divide them.

As they drank their coffee and waited for Mackenzie, Rose asked, "Have you heard from Lexi?"

Grace rolled her eyes in Rose's direction. "Really?" she asked.

Rose shrugged. "I was just asking. She didn't answer my calls. I just want to make sure she's okay, you know?"

"I'm sure she's fine," Grace said dismissively.

"I don't know, Gigi. You didn't see how she looked when she drove off. She's really hurt and angry."

Grace set her mug down. Rose pointing out the obvious was nothing new, but she understood it was only because Rose was genuinely worried. She was too, but she knew Lexi. She was stubborn and strong-willed. Once she got pissed, it'd be a while before she calmed down. Grace had called her a few times last night, not expecting her to answer but hoping she did. At least long enough for her to make sure she made it somewhere safe. Like everyone else, her call went straight to voicemail.

"I know," Grace said softly.

Rose sighed before asking, "If I ask you something, can you promise you won't get upset?"

Grace furrowed her brow, not willing to agree to those terms. "What is it?"

"Why didn't you tell her?"

"Tell her what?"

Rose peered over her shoulder to make sure Mackenzie wasn't behind them. She knew if she overheard them, she'd tell Alexis for sure. "About her father? Why didn't you tell her who it was?"

"It seemed like the right thing to do at the time," Grace leaned against the counter, "but I see now that it wasn't. I guess I was torn between her and Daniel."

"What do you mean torn between them? You don't owe Daniel any loyalty."

"Yeah, but I do owe him the truth. And although I had no intention of telling either of them now that it's out—I didn't want him to be ambushed."

"I don't understand why that would be your problem. Honestly, Lexi's feelings should be your priority. At the end of the day, who matters more to you? Daniel or Alexis?"

Grace stared at her. "I don't disagree with you, and of course, Lexi's feelings matter to me, but Daniel's feelings deserve to be considered too, don't you think?"

Rose tilted her head. "I guess… but do you think Lexi would've ambushed him?"

"I'm not sure, but I didn't want him to hear it from her. He deserves to hear it from me. She does, too, just not like this."

"Well, we know how Lexi is. Once she gets fixated on something, she won't stop until she gets what she wants. Which means you're on borrowed time."

"Tell me something I don't know," Grace said, gazing at her. "Speaking of borrowed time…."

Rose turned around to see Mackenzie sauntering angrily toward them. She didn't appear to be pleased, and they were sure they were about to get a piece of her mind.

"Which one of y'all want to explain to me why the hell Rose thought it was a good idea to wake me up? And rudely, nonetheless."

Mackenzie's hand was on her hip as she cut her eyes at them. She couldn't fathom what was so important they demanded of her presence especially since Grace had her own drama to deal with.

"Umm, hello?" She waved her other hand. "Somebody say something."

"Don't come down here with an attitude," Grace replied.

Mackenzie huffed. "Please, you'd have one too if you were woken up like that. Now what do y'all want? Otherwise, I'm going back to bed. I don't feel good, and I need my rest."

Rose and Grace glanced at one another.

"What's wrong with you?" Rose asked.

"Don't worry about it. It's not your business," Mackenzie snapped. The last thing she was about to do was tell them she was pregnant. She'd never hear the end of their mouths.

"Funny you said that since *your business* seems to always affect the rest of us," Grace spat.

"Gigi, you are the last person who should be talking. Your drama is the exact reason why this family is a hot mess right now. So please, spare me."

Mackenzie rolled her eyes. Grace arched her brow. She'd let her have that one. At least until they got what they needed to say off their chests.

"Is someone going to say something?" Mackenzie demanded.

Rose came right out and asked. "Who's Jasper?"

Mackenzie stood still as they watched the color drain from her face.

Rose had only asked the question because she wondered why Mackenzie hadn't told them she was married, but looking at her, they could see more to the story.

Grace said, "Mickey?"

She snapped out of her temporary shock and stared at them. The hairs on her arms stood at attention. How did they know? Who told them? Mackenzie's paranoia kicked in, and she glanced around as if she was being followed. "What did you just say?" she asked for clarification.

"I asked, who is Jasper?" Rose repeated.

Mackenzie reached behind her to lean against the wall. She suddenly felt as though her knees were going to give out and she needed something stable to hold her up. She parted her lips to let the heavy breaths escape before glancing back at them. "Where'd you hear that name?" she asked.

"Umm, no, you first," Grace replied.

Mackenzie diverted her attention to Rose. She was more reasonable. Mackenzie had no intention of entertaining Grace and her overbearingness.

"The sheriff," Rose answered, cutting to the chase. "He came by here yesterday and told us some man named Jasper Vincent filed a missing report in Atlanta for Mackenzie Vincent. The funny thing is we told him we didn't know anyone by the name of Mackenzie Vincent because his last name is Bayou. Imagine our surprise when he confirms you are indeed Mackenzie Vincent."

Grace folded her arms. "Start talking and fast. Otherwise, we're going to tell Mama you're married and on the run."

"We're concerned, that's all," Rose added, softening her tone in hopes of keeping things calm. "Mickey, if you need help, you can tell us. We're here for you."

Mackenzie appreciated Rose's concern, although it was a day late and a dollar short. She should have led with this instead of barging into her room, demanding she gets up like she was a child or something. Grace's body language projected a sense of entitlement that pissed her off all over again.

Mackenzie sneered at her and then straightened her stance. She pointed at Grace first, then Rose. "Let's get something straight, I don't owe either of you an explanation. The last time I checked, I was an adult. Who and what I do is my business. And Gigi, you have a child you should be worried about, and I'm not her."

Rose tightened her lips. That was a low blow even for Mackenzie. She closed her eyes and said a small prayer that Grace would take the high road... for once.

Grace stood silent, opting to let Rose handle this since anything that left her lips would result in her wrapping her hands around another of her sisters' necks.

"You're right, Mickey. You are grown, and you have a right to privacy. However, try and see things from our perspective. The sheriff shows up telling us you're *missing,* and we know you're not. Then to add insult to injury, he tells us you're married and have been for years. How do you expect us to react?"

"I'm not sure. I didn't really take your feelings into consideration with all that I have going on."

Mackenzie mulled over Rose's response. While she understood why they were questioning her, other people's feelings weren't at the top of her list at the moment. Aside from her own safety, she was worried about her friend. She'd called Nina a few times, and she hadn't responded. The stress of that alone superseded Rose and Grace's melodrama.

"So that's it? That's all you have to say?" Grace asked.

Mackenzie would've thought after yesterday's events, Grace might want to sit this one

31

out, but that'd be too good to be true. Her bossy nature was never too far away.

"Was there something else you were expecting to hear? Evidently, you know the gist of it. I'm married, end of story."

"End of story? How about you tell us why you're on the run?" Grace retorted.

"You and your self-righteousness are jokes," Mackenzie clapped back.

Grace was becoming agitated with her snarky comments. She knew something wasn't right when Rose and Alexis mentioned she showed up out of the blue.

"If you have something to say, just say it."

"I don't have anything to say because I mind my business. You should try it."

Grace tsked. "You know what, you're right, Mickey. You being on the run —is your business. But I'll tell you this, whatever is going on, you better keep it away from this house," she warned.

Rose winced. The authoritative way Grace said that was sure to get a reaction out of

Mackenzie. While they were on the verge of ripping each other's throats out, another thought crossed her mind. Why was Mickey hiding from her husband in the first place? What's going on that she felt she needed to not only run but keep her marriage a secret?

Mackenzie took a step forward, and Rose moved to intercept her. The last thing she wanted was another situation like the other day. Mackenzie was not Leslie at all. She would most certainly fight Grace back, and they'd tear the house up.

"Okay, let's take a breath," Rose advised.

"How do you have so much to say today, but yesterday's words were not your friend? Save all those threats for someone else because the way I see it, you have your own secrets to be concerned with."

"I'm a multitasker," Grace replied sharply.

"Whatever, I don't have to deal with this." Mackenzie turned to head toward her room.

"Mickey, wait," Rose pleaded. She knew her well enough to know that whenever she said something like that, it was only a matter of time before she fled again, and then they'd never find out what was going on with her. "Mickey, what has happened that you're running from this man?" she asked. "Did he do something to you? Are you in danger? Tell us something, please. We want to help."

Mackenzie flashed her a faint smile. She appreciated her sister's offer, but they couldn't help her. No one could. She had to fix this herself, and she couldn't do it here. She thought hiding out here would allow her the time to figure things out, but Jasper had raised the stakes. Reporting her missing meant she only had enough time to get out of there before someone confirmed her whereabouts, and he'd be on his way.

"Thanks Rosie, but I got it," she said, then disappeared down the hall.

Rose turned back around to see Grace sipping coffee that was cold by now. She loved her sister, but sometimes she wished she wasn't so direct and in your face. But Grace had always been that way. She didn't sugarcoat anything, even when sometimes sugar was needed.

"That went well," she said, moving to reheat her own coffee.

"What did you expect? Its Mickey being her usual private, evasive, and reckless self. I wasn't holding my breath for a straight answer. I mean, she didn't even tell us she was married."

Rose glanced at her. "You could've been a little gentler with her."

Grace rolled her eyes. "Maybe, but I meant what I said. Whatever is going on with her, she needs to keep it away from here."

"Do you think Lexi knows?"

"Probably. I wouldn't be surprised if she did. They tell each other everything, but trying to get anything out of her right now is not on the table."

"What about Leslie?"

Grace chuckled. "Seriously? We all know Leslie doesn't keep secrets."

Rose smirked at her response. If Grace only knew…. Leslie was very capable of keeping secrets—hers and other people, including the one Rose, had yet to tell.

"I don't know. She's kept yours all this time," Rose reminded her.

"Yeah, but at what cost? She's hung that over my head since we were young, and every time I come home, she doesn't let me forget it."

"I will say this, though. I'm ready to be done with all of this secrecy," Rose admitted. I just hope whatever Mickey is running from; she figures it out before it's too late… you, too."

Grace glanced over her mug at Rose. She knew what she had to do, but doing it was an entirely different story.

CHAPTER THREE

Leslie sat at her computer, scrolling through the course catalog as she finalized which classes she would be taking in the fall. She felt strangely inspired by everything that occurred—the discord in her marriage, her father passing then leaving them the inheritance. Finishing her degree had always been a dream of hers, and she was determined to do it more so now than ever. It'd been almost sixteen years since she'd been a student, and she was only fifty credit hours short before she withdrew.

During her sophomore year, she got pregnant with Myles. It was a slight adjustment in the beginning, but she made it work. Then a year later, she got pregnant with Micah. Juggling school, trying to work, and motherhood had begun to weigh on her heavily. Along the way, she'd gotten married, and Mathias was called to the pulpit.

Between being a wife, a mother, and the church responsibilities—school didn't fit into her life anymore.

Not to mention, Mathias gave so much of his time and attention to that church, among other things, he didn't bother to ask if she had goals and aspirations.

Though Leslie would never say she regretted being a mother, she did hold some discontent about the timing of it all. Every so often, fragments of regret or what-ifs would surface, and she'd have to stuff them back down. But that was the past. Now it was her time to do something for herself. And as much as she hated to admit it, despite Grace's delivery—she was right. Leslie was responsible for her own dreams and happiness, no one else.

She could blame Grace for leaving, but the truth was, she did what she wanted to do. All of them did. They all chose to pursue their dreams, so what was stopping her? Her marriage and children were the only obstacles because she allowed them to be.

"Where are you?" she mumbled, searching for the last class her advisor told her she would need.

She was majoring in Fine Arts with an emphasis on Interior Design along with some business courses. She wanted to soak up all the knowledge she could to ensure her business would succeed. Whether or not her sisters wanted to be a part of it, she was all in. Leslie desperately needed her own white whale, something that fulfilled her outside of making sure everyone else was taken care of.

She clicked the link. "There you are."

Her phone buzzed, interrupting her search. She glanced down at it to see it was a text from Rose.

Rose: Have you heard from Lexi?

Leslie stared at the text and wondered why she was asking about Lexi when the last she heard, all of them were at her parents' house. Leslie picked up her phone to reply, then returned her attention back to her task at hand. A few seconds passed before her phone vibrated again.

Rose: If you do, can you ask her if she made it back home safely?

Leslie sighed, curious as to why she was being used as a conduit between her sisters when Rose could just as easily pick up the phone and call Alexis herself. She had half a mind to call her and ask her that very thing, but she decided against it. She had other things to do. Important things. She glanced at the bottom of her screen and saw it was one in the afternoon.

Mathias had taken the kids with him since she was playing hooky from church, and knowing him, she didn't have much longer before her house became a madhouse again. The last thing she wanted to do was disrupt her peace and quiet with family drama. Her father's death was doing a number on her, and with having to plan everything and still be a parent, she was emotionally exhausted. In addition to that, she hadn't had a chance to grieve properly, and she desperately needed space too.

Whatever they had going on, they'd figure it out without her. She planned on discussing her return to school with Mathias once he got home. Part of her was dreading it since they hadn't been on the best of terms lately, but considering he'd taken ample time to be selfish, she couldn't care less how he felt. It was time he stepped up and did more around the house so she could chase her dreams.

Leslie smiled as she selected her last class and completed her registration. She was looking forward to obtaining her degree and building a business. Her circumstances had changed drastically, but with some focus and organization, everything would work out. Continuing on her euphoric high, Leslie opened Pinterest and dove into her virtual decorating and staging of their new event space.

She'd just purchased a new program that allowed her to stage spaces in 3D, and later on, she'd be paying a visit to the county courthouse to get the blueprints of the property so she could dive into reconstructing the space. Her uncle said he could do some of the work, but she knew he couldn't do all of that by himself, so she would have to look into hiring a construction company.

She also had a business plan on her list of things to do. Even if her sisters refused to contribute capital to the project, she'd be prepared to procure business loans and grants if she needed to. Maybe once she did that, they'd see how serious she was, and the stragglers holding out would get on board.

Her phone screen lit up again.

Rose:????

Leslie rolled her eyes and picked up her phone. Swiping left, she tapped Rose's name and held the phone up to her ear.

"Hello," Rose answered.

"Is there a reason you keep asking me Lexi's whereabouts? Why can't you call her and see if she's home? What's going on?" Leslie rattled off one question after the next. She waited a few seconds for a response then said, "Hello…are you there?"

"Are you done?" Rose asked.

Leslie huffed. "Yes."

"If I'm asking you to check on her, it's because she's not answering my calls."

"And why not?" Leslie lightly patted her foot against the hardwood. Her irritation was growing by the minute, and she wasn't ready to escape her happy bubble just yet.

Rose answered, "It's a long story, but let's just say she left pissed."

"About?" Leslie asked, unsure as to why Rose was leaving off pieces of the story when she was the one who opened the door.

"I'll tell you about it later."

Rose texting her a million times then having the nerve to be vague in her responses was annoying as hell.

"Fine, is that all?"

"Umm…" Rose murmured. "I guess so. You seemed to be in a hurry. Did I interrupt something?" she asked.

Leslie took a deep breath realizing she had come off a little snappy. "Sorry, I didn't mean to be extra snippy. I was putting together some ideas for the event space," she said, leaving off the fact she'd re-enrolled in school.

She wanted to tell Mathias before sharing the news with everyone else. However, having their support might make his reaction a lot easier to swallow.

"Oh wow. I'd love to see those," Rose answered excitedly.

"Hmm, I'll show you once I have everything put together."

"That works, too."

"Alright," Leslie said, ready to end the call. "I'll let you know if I hear from Lexi. And if I don't, I'll call her my—" Leslie turned her head at the knock on her door— "Rose, let me call you back. Someone's at my door."

As Leslie stood up, the person knocked again. Perhaps it was someone coming to check on her after church. It was almost two, which meant most services had let out. She peered through the peephole and saw long, brown hair. Not knowing who the woman was, she opened the door to a vixen.

Leslie's eyes roamed over the woman who could've been a body double for Jessica Rabbit. Her long, flowy brown hair hung in the middle of her breasts, and her pouty lips were nearly perfect. Full eyelashes curled up over almond-shaped eyes. The stretchy material that adorned her frame left little to the imagination.

She would've felt insecure had her eyes not shifted to the little girl, standing mid-thigh with the same color hair. By the looks of her, she was somewhere between four and six years old. Her head was stuck to the fullness of her mother's buttocks as she shyly hid behind her.

Leslie's stomach started to form knots, tightening with each breath she took. There was a familiarity in her features she couldn't ignore. Her eyes trailed back up at the audacious woman. The nauseating feeling, combined with her intuition, told her who she was without her ever speaking a word. She had nightmares about this very moment. She'd been the question mark, the disruption in her marriage. She swallowed, hydrating her throat that had dried.

"May I help you?" Leslie asked boldly. Her courage was hanging on by a thread, but she wouldn't let her know that. "Are you looking for someone in particular?"

"Yes, I'm looking for you," the woman responded.

Leslie arched her brow. "And you are?"

"Vanessa Tidwell," she replied, "The woman your husband had been having an affair with."

Leslie's heart dropped. She knew it. Still, the confirmation didn't hurt any less. She thought knowing the truth, and putting a face to her husband's deception would make it a little more bearable, but it didn't. At this moment, she realized not having a face to put to her agony was best. Now she had someone to measure her inadequacy. Now she had a name to obsess over.

Vanessa Tidwell, she thought.

Leslie crossed her. "What is it that you want, Vanessa?"

"I thought you'd want to know the truth."

"And what's the truth?"

******

Leslie sat facing the door. She was waiting for him. Heat raced through her body as she sorted through the events that had passed. It'd been three hours since Vanessa showed up at her door. She thought about calling him, but she didn't want to risk blowing up on him over the phone. This was not a conversation she wanted to have over the phone. No. This was something she had to look him in the face and talk about.

47

Next to her leg, she rocked back and forth, was a bag. As far as she was concerned, this was no longer his home, and he was no longer welcome. His disrespect had exceeded its limits. She'd tolerated it a lot and turned her head to a few things, but this wasn't something she would accept.

She picked up her phone.

Leslie: Where are you?"

Mathias: In the driveway.

She placed her phone down and straightened in the chair she'd been sitting in for the last hour. She wanted him to see the look on her face and the bag she packed for him the instant he opened the door. For the past two hours, she had rehearsed what she would say to her children when she sat them down and told them their father wouldn't be living here for a while—if ever again. Countless scenarios played over in her head as she built up her fortitude to do what needed to be done.

Leslie snapped out of her head when she heard multiple footsteps running up the walkway. Minutes later, the lock turned, and the door opened.

"Mommy!" the kids shouted as they trampled inside.

Leslie forced a smile as she kissed and hugged her children. She inhaled their sweet essences. Their hugs and squeezes comforted her.

"You all had quite the day, huh?" she asked.

"Yes!" they shouted in unison.

"Well, that's good to hear. Are you all hungry?"

"No, ma'am!" Lauren exclaimed. "Daddy already took us to get something to eat."

"Oh, he did, did he?" Leslie asked as her eyes landed on Mathias. He was still standing at the door, staring at the bag. She looked back at them. "What did Daddy feed you?"

"Nettie Bees," Myles blurted out.

"Hmm," Leslie said, not surprised. There weren't too many places he would eat at on Sunday. "Well, glad you're not hungry. How about you all go take those clothes off, change into something comfortable, and play in your rooms for a while? Mommy needs to talk to Daddy for a second."

They all nodded then ran off to their rooms.

When Leslie was sure they were out of sight, she turned back to the philandering man standing in front of her.

Mathias stared at her, trying to figure out what she was about to complain about this time.

Leslie kicked the bag toward him. Pointing to the table next to the door, she said, "Leave your key on the table right there. You don't live here anymore."

"What are you griping about now, Leslie?"

"No griping. Just me informing you that you no longer can stay here. Now, where you choose to lay your head is not my problem, but it won't be here," she replied matter-of-factly.

"Did you forget I pay the bills here? You don't get to tell me where I do and don't live."

"I don't think you heard me. Mathias, you will not be staying here tonight or any other night. Please, leave. I don't want the kids to hear us argue."

"Argue about what?" he asked, frustrated.

"Vanessa Tidwell."

His eyes almost jumped out of their sockets. His lips parted as he struggled to form words. That name was the last thing he expected her to utter. For five years, he'd kept those two worlds separate.

"Speechless?" she asked sarcastically.

Mathias blinked as he regained his focus. "W-W-What? Where did you hear that name?"

"Not who is that? Or perhaps, I don't know who that is, but where did I hear that name?" Leslie shook her head. "At least you aren't denying it."

"That wasn't a confirmation."

"It wasn't denial either. So yes, it was confirmation."

Mathias tucked his hands in his pockets. "Leslie…"

"Don't! Don't stand here and try to explain or excuse your actions. I already know everything. And here I am thinking you've only been cheating on me for a year, when in fact, it's been going on since before Zöe. Actually, it appears to have started up again right around the time you asked me about having another child. Tell me, was it because I said no, or did you at least come up with another reason to break our vows? Because I refuse to believe you would purposely impregnate another woman because I said no," she said, her voice cracking.

Mathias gazed at his mostly mild-tempered wife. The haunted look in her eyes shook him to his core. He had cheated on her multiple times but hadn't gotten anyone pregnant. In fact, the woman he was having an affair with at the moment was not Vanessa. He hadn't slept with her in years, and there was no way they could have a baby.

"Leslie, I have never gotten another woman pregnant. She is lying," he declared.

"She wasn't a baby. *She* looked to be around Zöe's age if not a little older."

Wait…what? Mathias thought. That was impossible.

"Leslie, she's lying. We haven't slept together in years."

Leslie swallowed as she trembled. Did he say years? As in…she wasn't the woman he was currently sleeping with?

Mathias realized what he said the instant his wife glared at him venomously. The contempt that layered the anger her face was flushed with confirmed it. He had stuck his foot in his mouth but was caught between a rock and a hard place. He had violated their vows, but he wasn't sloppy.

"I meant," he started to say.

Leslie rose calmly. "You don't have to explain anything, Mathis. Leave."

"I'm not leaving."

"Do you think it's safe to sleep here tonight? Get the hell out of my house," she screamed. "Now!"

CHAPTER FOUR

Mackenzie stared at her phone as it rang repeatedly. She'd been trying to contact Nina ever since Jasper caught them talking. Thoughts of what could've happened ran rampant across her mind.

The phone rang a few more times before she finally heard someone answer in a hushed tone, "Hello."

"Nina…Nina…is that you?" Mackenzie rambled.

"Mickey," she said softly.

Thank God, Mackenzie exhaled deeply.

Nina was whispering, which told Mackenzie her friend was sneaking to talk to her. She feared the worst again when she wondered if Jasper was near her. It wouldn't surprise her if he was keeping her on a tight leash. She had to ask without seeming too obvious.

"Press a button if you're at the shop," Mackenzie told her.

She waited, and nothing, so she moved on to her next question. If Nina pressed a button this time, she was going to hang up and call her later. She'd want to talk more, but not at the risk of Jasper or anyone else finding out. Mackenzie would rest somewhat, knowing she was at least able to hear her voice.

"Press a button if Jasper is in your vicinity."

Nothing. Mackenzie exhaled the breath she'd been holding. Hearing Nina was alone and okay relaxed her a little bit. She didn't want her friend to be hurt because of her.

"Nina, oh my God…I'm so glad to hear your voice. I was so worried about you."

"Yeah, I had to lay low for a second. Jasper wasn't happy to catch us talking, especially since I'd been telling him I hadn't heard from you."

"What happened? He didn't hit you, did he?" Mickey asked.

She didn't think Jasper would physically assault Nina in the shop, but she never thought he'd hit her either, so she had to ask.

"No, but it got ugly. He damn near tore up the shop in a rage. Screaming you stole from him, and if he couldn't get his money, he'd make you suffer. Mickey, he is losing it by the minute. I don't know what money he's talking about, but he is a lunatic on a mission."

"He reported me missing, Nina," Mackenzie confessed.

She heard Nina gasp. "That makes sense," she finally said. "It explains why he suddenly left town."

"What do you mean left town?"

"Mario told me Jasper had to leave town, but he didn't say where or why. I didn't really ask why since him being away meant he wouldn't be coming up to the shop, but it makes sense…he left looking for you."

Chills ran down Mackenzie's spine. He couldn't. There was no way he knew where she was, or did he? Did the sheriff call Atlanta PD and tell them she was here? Panic coursed through her veins. She had to get out of here, fast. The sheriff came to her house almost a week ago, meaning Jasper had a head start. Mackenzie's thoughts scrambled as she tried to come up with a plan. Where was she going to go now? Back to Atlanta?

No… maybe.

She could sneak back and lay low until she figured out her next move. The city was big enough, and since he already knew she wasn't in Atlanta, he wouldn't look for her there.

"The sheriff came to my parents' house…"

"About you?" she asked.

"Yes. Jasper filed a missing person's report on me."

Nina gasped. "What did your sisters tell the sheriff?"

Rose and Grace never said what they told him. She just assumed they confirmed she was there. And she would've thought to ask had they not been on their high horses trying to scold her.

"They probably told him I wasn't missing. I can't think of a reason why they wouldn't."

Mackenzie contemplated her own words as they left her lips. They had no knowledge of her being on the run or why she was hiding from Jasper, so telling him she wasn't missing would make sense. She sighed and rubbed her forehead frustratedly at her own secretness. If she had told them what was going on when she first arrived, they could've told him she wasn't here or at the very least, concocted a story that would've protected her. But now, considering everything—he probably went back and told Atlanta PD she was safe and sound in Deridder.

"I'd ask if I were you," Nina told her. "My gut tells me Jasper is headed your way."

She didn't have to. She knew Nina was probably right. If Jasper had left town, he was indeed looking for her. Otherwise, he'd be at the shop monitoring Nina's calls, making sure no one else was communicating with Mackenzie.

"Thanks," she said. "I have to figure out some things. Save this number, just not under my name. I'll call you in a few days."

"Okay. Be safe, Mickey. I'm serious."

Mackenzie disconnected the call and got out of her father's truck, then headed to Leslie's door. Not long after she'd gotten into it with Grace and Rose, she packed her bags and left. Mackenzie didn't care to have another dispute. The sheriff showing up didn't sit well with her either.

Now she had to contend with Jasper being on the hunt.

Mackenzie stepped onto the porch and knocked a couple of times. While waiting, she searched for reasons he would risk going to the police. He had to be pretty desperate to do that. Obviously, he wanted this money. Mackenzie gripped the strap of her duffel bag as she tried to figure out if Jasper would fly or drive.

Flying would make more sense, but then how would he get her back? How would he get the money back? He couldn't drag her through the airport; that'd draw too much attention. She heard someone yell and raise her hand to knock again when the door flung open, and her sister stood in

60

the doorway like a psychopath. Mackenzie looked behind Leslie to see Mathias staring like this was the worst time for her to show up.

"Leslie, what's going on?"

"What do you want, Mickey?"

Mackenzie opened the screen door—stepping forward—silently forcing Leslie back as she inched inside the house. She stumbled, almost tripping over something on the floor. Looking down, Mackenzie noticed a large duffel bag stuffed to the brim. Glancing at her sister, it didn't take a rocket scientist to see Mathias was getting kicked out.

"Did I come at a bad time?"

"What do you think?" Leslie answered sarcastically.

Mackenzie held her hands up in defense. Somehow, she'd jumped from the frying pan into the fire. She thought she'd get some peace and quiet coming here. "I just needed somewhere to crash tonight," she replied.

Leslie looked perplexedly at her younger sister. Her timing was horrible, as usual. If she was here, that meant something had gone awry over at her parents' house.

Everyone stood in silence as they exchanged awkward glances. Leslie redirected her focus to Mathias. Her sister showing up didn't change her decision regarding him staying here. Without saying a word, she picked up the bag, opened the screen door, and tossed it onto the porch. Mackenzie pursed her lips as she pretended to be invisible. She could hear the kids playing, oblivious to what was happening downstairs.

She wasn't sure whether or not she should give them some privacy or stand there in the event Mathias did something crazy. Leslie, on the other hand, seemed to be fully lucid and unafraid.

"I'm going to give you two some privacy; I'll be in the back until you finish."

"No need," Leslie said. She held the door open as she waved her hand, ushering Mathias out of it. "He was just leaving. Weren't you, Mathias?"

He looked between Leslie and Mackenzie, then back to his wife. The woman he betrayed and now his chicken had come home to roost. Prior to Mackenzie showing up, he had no intention of leaving, but her being here changed things. Leslie would for sure escalate things with an audience. And since he knew, Mackenzie would gladly rush to her sister's defense, he'd take the high road—tonight. Tomorrow was a different day.

Mathias walked past Leslie. "I'll be back tomorrow."

Leslie held out her palm and waited. He looked down then backed up at her. They resembled statues for a moment until he caved, reaching inside his pocket and retrieving his keys. He begrudgingly placed them in her hands.

"Don't come back here, Mathias. I mean it. Don't come until I call for you. Go deal with your other situation."

"Where am I supposed to stay?" he asked.

"Vanessa's." Leslie let the screen door close, before she slammed the front door in his face and locked it.

In no mood for company or entertainment. She turned to her sister. "Why are you here?"

"Who is Vanessa?" Mackenzie probed.

"You first," Leslie said, then headed toward her front room.

Following Leslie, she asked, "Do I need a reason to come by?"

Leslie flashed her a peculiar look as she headed to the couch to sit. "And how many times have you crashed at my house?"

"Good point." Mackenzie dropped the duffel bag inside the sofa chair next to her and sat down as well. Kicking her slides off, she swung her feet up and tucked them beneath her. "I had to get away from your sisters. They were driving me crazy."

Leslie rubbed her temple. They probably started interrogating her, and she got upset and flew the coup. "What'd they do now?" she asked.

Mackenzie waved her finger. "No, don't try to change the topic. What did I just walk in on? And why did you throw your husband out?"

"That's my business, and you're in my house. There has to be a reason you left our parents' home to come to this circus tent. So, start explaining."

"It's a long story. I don't even know where to start."

"That seems to be the phrase of the day." Leslie leaned forward to open the drawer and pulled out the lighter. Lifting the candle top in front of her, she lit it and did the same for the candle on the table next to her.

"What do you mean?"

"You...Rose...Vanessa...everyone seems to have interrupted my day with whatever drama you have going on."

"Rose called you?" Mackenzie asked, choosing not to address the fact that it was Leslie's second time mentioning that name.

"Yes, earlier. She was looking for Lexi. Something about her leaving pissed but she didn't exactly go into why."

"Let me ask you something; when you called Gigi a deadbeat mother, what did you mean by that?"

"Why do you ask?

"Did you call her a deadbeat mother because you knew about her being Lexi's biological mother?" she came right out and asked.

Leslie coughed a couple of times.

"What? How...where?"

"Lexi overheard Gigi and Mama talking about Gigi being her mother. They admitted once Lexi grilled them about it. So again, how long have you known?"

Sighing, Leslie admitted, "Since we were teenagers."

Mackenzie shook her head disapprovingly. It was wild to her that she and Lexi had been completely left in the dark. Although now, Leslie and Grace's rivalry made sense. Leslie felt some kind of way about how Grace abandoned her responsibilities while she got stuck with all the babysitting.

"Explains why you two stay into it."

"Yeah," Leslie answered solemnly, only recently acknowledging her anger had been misdirected.

"Who's the father?"

Leslie didn't hide her befuddlement. "Are you asking me because you're trying to confirm, or you really don't know?"

Mackenzie's silence told Leslie she had no idea.

Leslie laughed. "Grace is going to take that secret to the grave," she uttered.

"Then tell me. Gigi wouldn't tell Lexi after she asked several times."

Leslie considered it for a moment and decided against it. If Grace hadn't said anything, it wasn't going to come from her. She had her own issues to deal with and didn't want the blowback from overstepping again. Mackenzie would have to use her interrogation tactics on someone else.

"No, if Grace didn't tell her who her father was, then it won't come from me."

Mackenzie swiped her nose a few times and took a deep breath. "Really, Leslie? Of all people, you're the one to hold out. What if I promise not to tell her? It's not cool that y'all are doing this us versus them stuff."

"I'm staying out of it."

"But you've been in it," Mackenzie reminded her. "You've been taunting Gigi for years about it so no need to keep a lid on it now."

Mackenzie's mouth started to water. She swallowed hard before slowly exhaling. Trying her hardest not to inhale. Up to now, she hadn't had any inadvertent reactions to smells, but whatever those candle scents were, they weren't blending well. Mackenzie moved her head side-to-side, gradually forcing the bile back down.

"What's wrong with you?" Leslie asked, noticing that she looked queasy.

Mackenzie exhaled. "Nothing."

Leslie didn't quite believe her, but she moved on. "As I was saying, I'm not getting involved with any of that. Grace is going to have to work that out for herself."

Mackenzie sat back. The scents stirred her stomach and revved it up even more. Inhaling and exhaling slowly was buying her time, but the more she breathed, the more nauseated she felt. Clawing the cushion next to her, Mackenzie took another long swallow.

"What's that smell?" Mackenzie asked assertively.

"What smell?"

Just as she was about to answer, Mackenzie darted toward the kitchen. Lowering her head, she vomited profusely in the large trash can until it felt like her stomach was empty and she was left dry, heaving. To her right, she heard the faucet turn on and off. Convinced there was nothing else left to regurgitate, she straightened and wiped the corners of her mouth.

Leslie held out a glass of water and asked, "How far along are you?"

Accepting the water, Mackenzie held the glass to her lip and took a few gulps. The cool water was refreshing. She drank slowly while trying to figure out how to breeze past her presumption.

"Who said I was pregnant?"

"Don't insult my intelligence, Mickey. I get enough of that from Mathias. Besides, do you think someone who has—" Leslie held up her hand and spread her fingers apart— "four kids don't know what pregnancy symptoms look like? Not to mention, you've been slightly moodier than your usual self. Be for real."

"I don't know," Mickey told her, pulling out one of the stools. "I found out the day of Daddy's funeral."

Leslie crossed her arms. "How long have you had morning sickness?"

"It just started."

"Are you keeping it?"

Mackenzie shrugged nonchalantly. "I haven't thought that far ahead."

"Why wouldn't you?"

"There's a lot to unpack there. Too much for tonight and we've taken up enough time talking about me," Mackenzie admitted. "Who's Vanessa?"

"My husband's mistress and possibly the mother of his bastard child."

Eyes widening, she was sure her ears had to be playing tricks on her. She processed the words, Leslie's aura, and what she walked in on. Then there was the extra emphasis she put on calling her a *bastard* child. Mathias being put out made sense now. Though truthfully, him being a player didn't seem too far off. He had a reputation for being one when they were younger.

Same for his brothers. Guess he hadn't strayed too far from it. Being a big-time minister didn't make him more faithful. Oddly, women flocked to ministers—married ministers—to do the most sinful things. It was quite an oxymoron.

Mackenzie wasn't an angel by any means, but even that was crossing the line for her.

Her sister appeared stoic. She wanted to offer her some advice, but she had none to give. Her family was imploding, and it was like every which way she turned; it collapsed a little bit more.

CHAPTER FIVE

"Aww come on," Grace grumbled.

She fumbled with the corkscrew as she wiggled it inside of the cork. Grace hated it when she didn't stick it in the right because that meant she'd end up tearing the cork up before she finally got it. Her phone buzzed, and she took a break to look and see who it was. She'd informed her team she would be heading back soon, so it was probably something being put on her calendar.

Illuminating her screen, she saw it was a text from Daniel asking if she was free.

Grace had been avoiding him since the blow-up with Alexis. She knew telling him was necessary, but she wasn't necessarily rushing to do it. They'd reconnected and being around him unlocked something inside she hadn't felt in a long time. She never quite got over how they ended. But

73

telling him about Alexis right now meant she could lose him again, and she wasn't ready to do that yet.

Swiping her screen, Grace tapped his name and waited as the phone rang.

"Hello, Grace Bayou," he greeted, his baritone comforting. "I was expecting a simple text. Imagine my surprise to get a phone call."

Grace chuckled as she shook her head. "Very funny. Now why are you asking if I'm free?"

"I would like you to be free Thursday evening around seven so that I can take you to dinner before I head back to New Orleans on Friday. That is if you aren't leaving before then."

Grace contemplated his request. His leaving so soon didn't give her much time to tell him about Alexis. She'd need a few more days to prepare herself for this catastrophe and the possibility he would probably never speak to her again, let alone forgive her.

"Leaving already huh?" she asked.

"Yeah, I split my time between my practices here and there. And since I've already been here a couple of weeks, it's time to check on that location. I also miss Sydney," he said.

Grace could feel him smiling through the phone.

"I understand. It's time I head back to L.A. myself."

"So, is that a yes?"

Grace smiled. "Yes. I will join you for dinner."

"Then it's a date. Shall I pick you up, or do you want to meet there?"

Grace mulled over his question. Telling him and then having to ride home in the same car would probably be a little awkward. Not to mention it was highly unlikely he'd even want to be near her after hearing the truth.

No, she'd drive herself.

"Let's meet there," she replied casually.

He laughed. "Scared I might kidnap you?"

Grace joined him, laughing at his playful jab. "I'm not worried about being kidnapped since everyone will know where I'm going and who I'm with; you won't get far," she teased.

"Always the cautious one."

"Only way to survive. Back to our dinner, where am I meeting you?"

Grace peeked around the wood column after hearing a car door slam loudly. She assumed it was Mickey returning from wherever she'd run off to, though she figured she'd be halfway across the country by now. Surprisingly, sticking around wasn't her thing either and was something they had in common. She'd brought their father's truck back yesterday but hadn't bothered coming inside. Grace assumed she was still pissed and decided to crash at Leslie's house another night.

"What are you in the mood for?" he asked, pulling her attention back to their conversation.

"I'm not a picky eater so you choose."

"How about 19 Candles?"

Grace laughed at his choice. "Fine with me, big spender."

"Oh really?"

His suave chuckle tickled her ear but was quickly interrupted by the ringing doorbell. A wrinkle formed in her forehead, and she wondered why Mackenzie didn't just use her key. When the doorbell rang again, Grace knew her youngest sister was being a brat. She sighed annoyingly.

"Did I say something wrong?" Daniel asked.

"No...no...I'm sorry. That wasn't for you. It was in response to my bratty sister. Now back to you, big spender...."

"You're worthy of a five-star meal, so I don't mind."

Grace shivered. There was something about the velvety way the words rolled off his tongue that sent shivers down her spine. She was doing her best to keep it together despite how badly she wanted to test the waters and see if it was better than she remembered.

"Why thank you," she blushed.

"You're more than welcome."

The doorbell rang again.

"Daniel, let me call you back," she told him.

"Okay, let's talk later."

Grace ended the call and sashayed across the room. "Mickey, why th—" Stopping mid-sentence when she saw it wasn't her sister, she was brought up short. Before she stood a well-dressed man she'd never seen before. "May I help you?" she asked.

"Good afternoon. Is this the Bayou residence?"

Grace stared at him as she processed his question. He was incredibly handsome and definitely not from around these parts. His accent also gave it away though she couldn't quite place where it was from.

"Depends on who's asking." She narrowed her eyes. "How can I help you?"

"I'm looking for Mackenzie Bayou. I was told this was her family's house."

"And you are?"

Jasper grinned, then gently placed his hand on his chest, shifting to his more charismatic side. "Apologies, my name is Jasper, and your sister is my wife," he informed her. "I was told this was her parents' house."

Grace was immovable as the words left his lips. The sheriff had shown up less than a week ago, informing them that Mackenzie had a husband, and there he was in the flesh. Grace hadn't quite formed a picture of what he might look like, but if she were to create a visual based on Mackenzie's prior relationships; he fit the description.

"Are you her mother or one of her sisters?" Jasper asked.

Grace bypassed his inquiry. "How can I help you?"

She wasn't about to volunteer any information. Even though the earlier conversation with her and Mackenzie didn't end on the best note, she couldn't help but remember Rose's questions and wonder the same thing. Why was Mackenzie running from him?

Jasper noticed the resemblance between her and Mackenzie. If he were to imagine an older Mackenzie, she would look like Grace. He wondered how old she was since Mackenzie was twenty-nine. There had to be at least a fifteen-year difference since he knew it was five of them.

"I hate that we are meeting this way, but I'm looking for your sister. She left almost two weeks ago—no notice—no anything, and I've been waiting for her to call or show up."

"Have you called the police?" she asked knowingly. While waiting for a response, Grace leaned against the doorframe, unsure if she would invite him in.

"I did. I waited for two days, and when she didn't call or come home, I filed a report."

Grace got straight to the point. "Jasper, why would my sister disappear for two weeks and not call her husband? I mean, what kind of wife would do that?"

She had no idea what was going on between Mackenzie and her husband; however, people didn't ghost their significant other for two weeks if something troubling wasn't going on. And before she invited him in, she needed to know if he was a threat to her sister and their family.

"May I come inside?" he asked politely.

"I'm still deciding, so how about you answer my questions first? Then I'll let you know."

Jasper looked away briefly to hide his irritation. He rubbed his fingers across the stubble that had grown on his jaw. Her sister's third-degree vexed him, and he couldn't help but wonder what his beloved wife had told them about him. In a town this small, he was sure the sheriff had already come by and told them a report was filed.

It had taken him a minute to remember, but he eventually recalled where she said she'd grown up and notified Atlanta PD. A few days later, he got a call from them stating that the county sheriff's office had verified she was indeed here and had been on account of their father's passing. He was in his car before the call ended.

"To be honest, your sister and I have had a rough couple of months, but what married couple doesn't. I guess after our last argument, she needed some time apart. I thought she checked into a hotel to cool off, but when she didn't show up after another day or two, and then her number was disconnected, I got worried."

Grace wasn't sure how true the first part of his response was, but she knew he wasn't lying about her number being disconnected. She remembered Rose…or Leslie mentioning something similar when they called her.

"There's a big difference between skipping town and cooling off for a few days," she pointed out.

"Depending on the person, it could be one in the same," he refuted.

Just as Grace was about to challenge his statement, she heard footsteps behind her. "Gigi, did I hear the doorbell ring?"

"Yeah, Ma. I got it," she answered. She didn't want to lie to her mother, but until she vetted him and warned Mackenzie, she wanted to keep her mother in the dark. "Just someone looking for Mickey."

"Well, who is it?" she asked.

Grace hesitated for a few seconds before deciding to let the man in. Jasper took a couple of steps back. Once she had it opened far enough, he stepped around to walk inside.

"Come in," she said dryly.

Aurelie looked at the man entering her house, assuming Grace knew who he was since she opened the door for him. She leaned against one of the plush chairs situated in her front room. The screen door shut behind him.

"Gigi, who is this?"

Grace closed the door and moved to stand next to her mother. There was no way she could cover it up now. "Ma, meet Jasper Vincent—" she crossed her arms while staring at her sister's secret husband — "Mickey's husband."

CHAPTER SIX

Grace and Rose sat in the chairs across from their mother and Jasper. After she dropped the bomb on her mother, Rose joined them. Immediately after their mother offered him a seat, Grace whispered to Rose who the man was.

Upon hearing it, Rose fought like hell to keep her lips closed. She'd have to grin and bear the sudden shock. He looked a little older than Mackenzie did, but she saw the appeal.

Aurelie's cheeks flushed with disappointment as her brows creased. Hundreds of thoughts rushed through her head. None of which made sense. She had so many questions but couldn't figure out where to start.

"Excuse me for being frank, but there's no way my daughter is married, and we don't know about it," Aurelie said, then looked at her daughters as if for confirmation.

Grace kept a straight face. Neither of them had gotten around to telling their mother the sheriff showed up the other day, nor had they told her that Mickey had recently admitted she was married.

"I understand, Mrs. Bayou," Jasper said, "but it's the truth. And I was under the impression all of you knew. I know we ran off and eloped, but she told me that all of you knew."

Jasper remained calm despite how furious he was beneath the surface. Finding out that Mickey had lied, and he'd been kept a secret from her family stung.

Aurelie shook her head. "No. We've never heard of you or anything about Mackenzie being married."

Rose glanced at Grace. She wondered at what point Grace was going to intercede and tell her mother what they knew.

"Can you tell me how long you've been married to my daughter?"

"Four years," he told them. "We got married on New Year's Eve in Las Vegas."

Grace shook her head. Surprisingly, Mickey eloping in Vegas was befitting. If she had to pick any of them to elope and do it in secret, it'd be Mackenzie.

Their mother's eyes widened as she turned to look at Grace and Rose. "You two knew about this?"

Grace sighed internally. "Mickey hasn't mentioned anything about a husband to me."

Rose shrugged. "Not a word. I need a drink. Does anyone else want anything to drink?" she asked, wanting to get out of the line of fire.

"No, I'm fine," Aurelie answered.

Grace gave Rose a look. They'd both just lied to their mother.

"I'd like some water if that's okay?" Jasper replied.

Rose flashed him a faux grin. She couldn't put her finger on it, but something about all of this didn't feel right.

Aurelie studied the man. "Why now? After four years, why have you decided to show up now? And why isn't Mackenzie here with you?"

Rose returned with his water and her drink. She passed the glass to him, placing a coaster down, then retook her seat.

"I haven't heard from her in two weeks."

"Why is that?"

Jasper was growing irritated with the interrogation. They were relentless; all he wanted was for them to tell him whether she was here or not, and he'd be gone. He thought leading with them being married would encourage her family to be more forthcoming. He was trying to decide whether or not they were stalling.

"We had a blowup, and it escalated," he lied.

Aurelie stared at him. "Escalated; how exactly?"

"Typical marriage issues," Jasper brushed off. "Nothing that would warrant her to leave the state and not tell me."

The three of them stared at him blankly.

"That's not telling me anything," Aurelie added.

He said, "I'd rather not go into details. Seeing as though it's our personal business."

Rose scoffed at his evasiveness.

"This is my last resort. I'm worried about her. She's never been gone this long."

"Mackenzie isn't missing. Matter of fact, where is she? I saw the truck was back?" Aurelie gazed at Grace.

"Ma, she brought that truck back late last night, but she never came in. I can only assume she's left again, "Grace said.

"Well, do you know where she is?"

"I don't." Turning to Jasper, she said, "How about you leave your information, and once I get ahold of her, I'll let her know you stopped by and to give you a call." Grace didn't trust the man and wanted to give her sister a heads-up just in case. She had an idea where she might be, though. There weren't too many places she'd flee to.

Jasper picked up the glass and finished his water. He didn't believe for one second that none of them knew where Mackenzie was, but he'd play along. He was in unfamiliar territory and didn't want to do anything to draw attention to himself or the fact Mackenzie had close to half a million dollars of his money. He'd play this smart.

Standing, he smiled. "I appreciate that. Take my number down."

Grace patted her pocket for her phone and remembered she'd left it on the counter. She asked Rose, "Do you have your phone?"

"No, I left it in my room."

"Write it here," their mother said, taking a small notepad out of the coffee table drawer, and placing a pen down on top of it. "How long do you plan to be in town?"

"As long as it takes to fix things with Mackenzie."

Jasper scribbled down his information. Doing a quick scan of the room, he didn't see any shadows lurking, indicating Mackenzie was somewhere hiding and listening, so he walked to the door where Grace stood holding it open.

"Nice to meet all of you. Once again, I hate that it was under these circumstances, but I'm glad I got a chance to meet everyone," he told them.

Grace gave something of a smile. "As soon as we get ahold of Mackenzie, we'll tell her to call you.

Jasper nodded and walked out. He wasn't expecting to hear from them which was why he wasn't going far. Mackenzie wasn't about to slip through his fingers again.

CHAPTER SEVEN

Alexis sat staring at the computer. Her shift had been pretty quiet, with the exception of one of her patients coding, but now things were back to normal. She thought picking up an extra shift would help to keep her mind off her problems, but it really didn't. Her phone had been blowing up since she left, but she had no desire to talk to anyone. She didn't want to hear more lies or deal with people avoiding her questions.

"What's got you lost in thought?" her co-worker Erica asked.

Alexis snapped out of her daze. "Nothing and everything," she said, typing in the rest of the website address. She had decided to take Keith's advice and do a little digging for herself.

"You sure? You've been like a zombie since you came back. I'm sure Marilyn wasn't expecting you to come back so soon."

Marilyn was Alexis' supervisor and just so happened to be as surprised as everyone else when she showed up a couple of days ago.

"I'm fine," Alexis assured her. "A lot has happened these past two weeks. I just need to get my thoughts together."

"If you want to talk about it, you know I'm here."

Alexis flashed her a faint smile. She appreciated the concern, but sharing her family drama with coworkers was not something she cared to do. Keith knowing was enough. He'd already checked on her more times than she could count ever since she told him. His smothering was enough. She'd heard enough within these walls to know she didn't want to be at the center of people's breakroom gossip.

"Thanks, I appreciate it, but I'm good."

Erica nodded, then turned around to finish her charting, allowing Alexis to finish her task. Typing in *county records in Deridder,* she hit enter and waited for her results to pop up. Seconds later,

Beauregard Parish Courthouse was at the top of the list. She peeked over her shoulder to make sure Erica wasn't snooping and gradually dimmed her screen's brightness.

Her deep dive continued when she located the public records link and typed in her information.

No search results found.

"What?" she thought, double-checking what she input to make sure she didn't enter something wrong. "*What does that even mean?"*

Alexis erased what she put in the search boxes, retyped it, and then pressed enter again. After a few seconds, the same message as before appeared again. She racked her brain, trying to figure out how that was even possible. Taking a different approach, she entered Mackenzie's information. Without hesitation, a hyperlink with her name appeared. In the column next to it was her birthdate.

Alexis did the same for the others, finding the same results. So why was hers not showing up?

Annoyance consumed her. Locating the number at the courthouse, she picked up the phone and dialed.

The automated recording came on, and she listened until hearing the option she needed and selected that prompt. As the phone rang in her ear, Alexis glanced around again to make sure no one was listening and found Erica had slipped away. That was a superpower of theirs; all of the nurses had a way of disappearing without anyone hearing or seeing. Otherwise, they'd never enjoy a break without interruption.

"Hi, thank you for calling the Beauregard Parish Courthouse. This is Darla. How may I help you today?"

"Hi Darla, my name is Alexis Bayou, and I'm trying to locate my birth records on your site, but it keeps giving me a 'no search results found' message. Any reason why that would pop up?"

"There could be a few reasons. Let me see what I can do. Can you give me your full name and date of birth?"

"Sure," Alexis replied, rattling off her information. In between, she continued to check her surroundings.

"Miss Bayou, I do not see any birth records for you. And to be sure, you were born in Deridder, correct?"

"Yes," she said.

She could hear Darla pecking away at the keys and suddenly felt flushed. Something was off. All of her sisters—or her aunts—whatever they were, their information didn't take this long to come up. Alexis exhaled a frustrated breath as the tension slowly formed in the center of her face. She wondered if Bayou was the last name she was born under.

"Alright, so it seems the message you received was correct. I'm not sure why, though."

"Me either. I entered my siblings' information in, and theirs popped up," Alexis informed her.

She hummed. "That's odd, actually. Would you mind if I placed you on a brief hold right quick? I want to check and see if my supervisor can tell me what's happening."

"Yes, that's fine."

While Alexis waited, she felt her phone buzz against her left breast. Retrieving it, she saw it was a text from Keith. Since she returned, they'd been spending more time together. Alexis wasn't sure if it was because he'd finally gotten past her defenses or if it was because she didn't want to be alone with the voices and thoughts running amuck in her head.

Either way, he distracted her and made her feel good while doing it. Alexis replied to his text and slipped the phone back into her pocket.

"Hello, Miss Bayou?" Darla said, coming back to the phone.

"Yes."

"So, I spoke with my supervisor, and the only explanation he had for your records not showing up is because you weren't born in Deridder."

Alexis blinked rapidly. If not Deridder, then where was she born? Frown lines formed in her forehead. This was another obstacle in her quest to learn the truth.

"I'm sorry, that can't be right. My entire family, except for my parents, was born in Deridder. There has to be a mistake in your system somewhere."

"I thought that too, but I had him do an advanced search, and nothing popped up. If you were born in Louisiana, it wasn't in Deridder."

Alexis groaned internally. "Are you sure?"

"Positive, I triple-checked. A few of us did."

Massaging her temple, Alexis tried to think. Where did the copy she had come from then? If there was no record of her birth in the county records, that meant the copy she had was fraudulent. Now that she thought about it, she never really examined it. She just assumed it was real and the information on it was correct. All this time, after school, obtaining her driver's license, applying for jobs—all of it had been done with a fake birth certificate.

She was living her worst nightmare.

"Perhaps you can check the original document," she suggested.

That's not happening, Alexis thought to herself. Grace was guarding her paternity like it was the holy grail; telling her the location of her birth wouldn't be any easier to extract from her.

"I don't have it," Alexis lied, "It's why I'm trying to get another copy."

"I understand," Darla replied, empathizing with her. "But there's nothing I can give you. You could probably try and do a statewide search. If that doesn't work, I would ask your parents if you were born here. They'd be the only people who could point you in the right direction."

Alexis sighed. This was going nowhere fast.

"Is there anything else I can help you with?" Darla asked.

"No, that's all." Alexis didn't bother hiding her disappointment. "Thank you for your help."

"Anytime. Good luck with your search."

Alexis thanked her again and hung up the phone. She leaned back, lolling her head over the back of the chair as she figured out her next move. Her phone vibrated again, reminding her that she was supposed to be meeting Keith. She needed to find someone to sit at the desk before she disappeared. Poking her head into several rooms, she stumbled upon another colleague.

"Hey, Tera, I'm going to run to the cafeteria really quick. Can you keep an eye on things for me?"

Tera nodded. "Sure, go get something to eat. I got you."

"Thanks; I shouldn't be too long."

"Take your time; it's pretty slow."

Alexis smiled and walked off. Keith had his own office, and some midday fooling around could possibly lift her spirits. Pressing the elevator button, she waited until the doors opened. Right as she pressed the button to his floor, her phone rang.

When she checked her phone to see who was calling, she huffed, seeing it was Leslie. Debating whether or not she would answer, she stared at the phone for a few seconds.

"How can I help you?" she answered rudely.

"Dang, is that how you greet people when they call to check on you?" Leslie asked.

"What do you want, Leslie? I'm at work."

"Well, for starters, what's with the attitude? I didn't wake up to you this morning."

Alexis rolled her eyes as the elevator stopped and doors opened. Stepping out of it, she made her way toward Keith's office.

"You did, however, lie to my face my entire life, so I guess some attitude is warranted, don't you think?" Silence greeted her. Alexis paused and stepped to the side. Leaning against the wall, she said, "Exactly."

"Lexi…"

"No, don't even say anything especially if it's not the truth. I've been lied to enough."

"And how is that my fault?"

"Spare me, Leslie."

"I didn't lie to you."

"You didn't tell me the truth either, so as far as I'm concerned, omission is the same as lying."

"Lexi, it wasn't my place to tell you."

"Yet you felt the need to throw it up in Gigi's face every chance you got," she retorted.

"It still wasn't on me to say anything. Mama and Daddy would've killed me," Leslie said.

"Were any of you ever going to tell me the truth, or were you going to let me go the rest of my life believing Mama and Daddy were actually my parents?" Alexis felt her temper rising and took a few deep breaths to calm herself. This was not a conversation she wanted to have at work.

"Have you talked to Mama? From my understanding, she's worried—Rose, too."

Alexis scoffed at the mention of them being concerned. "So now everyone is worried about me? Where was all this concern thirty years ago? Matter of fact, where was it a week ago? You're just now calling me!" Alexis's voice rose a decibel, and she realized she needed to calm down.

Leslie understood her hostility given the circumstances, but she wasn't about to be Alexis' punching bag. She had enough to deal with in her own life.

"I'm sorry that I wasn't able to put my life on hold for you," she snapped. "I've had my own issues to deal with, but I am calling now."

Alexis's eyes narrowed. "Then I have two questions. Who is my father, and where was I born?"

Leslie sighed audibly in Alexis's ear. She had just told Mackenzie she was staying out of it, but hearing the hurt in Lexi's voice forced her to rethink that decision. Alexis deserved to know the truth, and now that the cat was out of the bag—she saw no point in keeping it a secret any longer.

"What is it?" Lexi asked impatiently. "Was she raped? Molested? Was he married? Is he dead? Was the man a criminal or something? Why is the question of my paternity being treated like classified information?"

"No, she wasn't attacked or anything like that. Lexi, I'm going to tell you the truth, but you better not say one thing to Grace or anyone else.

This is for your ears only. I better not hear from anyone that I told you," Leslie insisted.

Alexis brushed off her threat. "Whatever."

"I'm serious, Alexis. Not even Mickey. Promise me you won't say anything."

"You really expect me not to reach out to him?"

"I meant regarding Mama and the rest of them. But just so you know, Grace wasn't lying when she said he doesn't know, so you need to approach that situation delicately."

"He knew she was pregnant right?"

"Yes, he did. However, he's under the impression you were given up for adoption."

Adoption? She thought. First, it was her parents who weren't her parents, and now she's discovering she was allegedly put up for adoption. It was just one lie after the next. Alexis tossed Leslie's words around in her head. Even if that were the case, he had to give up his rights for Grace to do that, so that meant he was equally to blame for all of this.

"So, you're telling me he never came around after everything? Did he and Gigi break up after she had me? How were our parents able to pop up with a kid all of a sudden, and nobody questioned it? You don't think that's odd?" she asked.

"Lexi, do I think it's odd now that I have children? Yes. However, I was around ten or eleven at the time. So, I can't answer all those questions for you. That really is a conversation you need to have with Grace or Mama. What I can tell you is that I don't recall him coming around as much after they brought you home. And shortly after they graduated, Grace broke up with him and left town. I only know that because a couple of days later, he came looking for her, but Daddy told him she'd already left for school. I didn't see him much after that since he left for college too."

"They went to school together then?"

"Yes, they were high school sweethearts. He came to the funeral," Leslie told her.

Alexis searched her mind for who would've been there she didn't recognize then it dawned on her. There was a man there who'd helped Grace when she passed out.

"Wait a minute," she said, replaying that day back. "Was he the guy who carried her in the house? The one checking to make sure that she was okay?"

"Yep, that's him. His name is Daniel Alexander."

Alexis straightened at the mention of his name. This whole time, she'd been carrying a piece of him around and didn't know it. Grace had all but given her his name, except she never knew it.

"My name," she mumbled. "Alexis Danielle...she gave me his name."

Leslie didn't utter a thing as Alexis put the pieces together. She was extremely intelligent, so she knew the minute she mentioned his name, the similarity to Alexis' middle name would click. Now that she'd told her, Leslie would return to minding her business.

"Thank you, Leslie. Thank you for telling me the truth."

"You're welcome."

"I need to go," she said softly.

Leslie replied, "Okay. But if you need to talk about it or anything, call me."

"I will."

CHAPTER EIGHT

Rose gazed out the window as the miles of vacant land scattered between farms and exits. She had avoided her personal issues long enough. With all her sisters had going on, she'd almost forgotten about her own problems. It was time to rip the band-aid off.

Detective Graves had called several times, and she had booked and rebooked her flight countless times, and finally, she decided not to cancel again. She was avoiding the inevitable, that much she could admit. The truth of the matter was she wasn't sure she was ready to face Lucien.

Rose had played the *'what if'* game so many times in her head and still came up empty. She couldn't find a single reason why he would hurt her like this, and now she had to be the one to put him behind bars. She wasn't sure if that would make her feel better since she hadn't felt much relief since she learned he'd been arrested. However, she couldn't allow him to do this to another woman, no matter how much her heart ached.

"What's got you so quiet over there?" Grace asked.

"Just thinking about everything that happened, along with all the stuff I need to do when I get back."

"Yeah, we've all been off for a while now. I'm sure getting back to work will give us some kind of normalcy."

Normalcy...what was that? Rose asked herself silently. Her normal had been doused in gasoline and set ablaze. She was headed back to the remnants of that disaster.

"Yeah..." was all she could say. She hadn't quite gotten around to telling Grace she'd been handed her walking papers. Even though those papers came with a huge check, she couldn't deposit it because she had to close her account and open another one.

"I'm surprised you actually didn't have your phone glued to your ear the entire time," Grace teased. "You're normally always working on some major project."

Rose grinned to keep from lying. She peered back out of the window. "Guess they realized I needed a break."

"And you're sure I can't talk you into staying?" Grace asked, glancing over at her.

She laughed. "Not likely."

"Aww Rosie, plleaassee," she playfully pleaded. "Stay a little longer… until the weekend?"

"I'll be back, although I'm sure you won't be here when I do, or will you?"

Rose flashed Grace a questionable look. She knew with her leaving, Grace would be on the first plane out of Deridder. Alexis had already run off. Knowing Mackenzie, it wouldn't be long before she did too.

Rose had booked her flight back to Houston, saying she had some things to get back to. She didn't specify why, and Grace didn't have the energy to question her. Rose typically played things close to the chest anyway.

"That's a possibility," Grace replied, keeping her focus on the road. "I have to get back to L.A. I miss normal heat and the beach."

"And the fact that you'll be far away from Deridder helps, I'm sure." Rose smiled, shaking her head. She was actually more surprised Grace had been here this long. "Have you reached out to Daniel or Lexi yet?"

Grace stared ahead. "I spoke to Daniel the other day."

Her dry reply told Rose all that she needed to know.

"And?" Rose asked.

"We're supposed to be going to dinner tomorrow," she said.

"Is that when you plan on telling him?"

Grace shrugged undecidedly. "I don't know."

Grace took the ramp that led to the airport, exiting the highway. She had an hour drive back to figure out how and what she was going to say to him since was slated to leave tomorrow.

"He's headed back to New Orleans on Friday. I really didn't want to drop a bomb like that on him right before he leaves."

Rose chuckled. "You don't want to tell him at all, so don't let that be your excuse. Cat's out the bag now, Gigi, so put your big girl panties on and do what you need to do. Because this is not going away, and it's going to be a lot worse if Lexi shows up at his doorstep and tells him herself."

Grace pressed down on the brake, shifting the car into park once they arrived at the airport. She leaned her head against the headrest and stared out of the windshield.

"How would she do that? She doesn't know anything," Grace reminded her.

"You must've forgotten that there are two other people who do know—Mama and Leslie."

Grace turned her head in Rose's direction. She knew her mother wouldn't say anything, but she had forgotten about Leslie.

"Do you think Leslie would tell her?"

Rose shrugged. "I don't know. I mean, she probably won't, considering how things went the last time you two had it out, but if Lexi plays the sympathy card…who's to say."

Grace glanced out the side of her window. She knew Alexis would try to find as much information as she could.

"Trust me, I have a little more time."

Rose fumbled around in her seat, gathering her items, then opening the door. "That's what you thought about not revealing you're her birth mother, and you see where that got you." Rose leaned over to hug her sister. "I'll call you when I make it back to Houston."

Rose climbed out of the car and walked to the trunk to get her bags. Once she had everything, she closed the door and peeked back inside of the window. "And call Leslie, too. I'm sure by now she's heard from Lexi."

Grace scowled and rolled her eyes. "Why do I need to do that?"

"Don't be like that. You two need to let that go. Besides, one of us needs to tell Mickey her husband is looking for her since she's not answering *our* calls." Rose tapped on the door, "I'll call you later."

*****

Rose turned the key and opened the door, flicking the light switch on as she walked inside. Her house almost resembled how it first looked when she had just moved in. Standing here now, she was reminded of all she'd lost. She'd spent months searching for pieces and putting together the perfect decor for her home, and it was all for nothing.

Vexation coursed through her as she grabbed the handle and rolled her suitcase to her bedroom. It was the only room that he didn't steal from. Rose wasn't sure if that was luck or if he hadn't quite returned to finish the job. Either way, she was glad she had somewhere to lay her head.

She was exhausted in more ways than she could count. A hot bath and her bed were the perfect remedy. Tomorrow, she'd have to work on fixing her own life.

Pulling out her phone, she sent Grace and her mother a message letting them know she made it home, then one to Lexi. She knew she probably wouldn't respond, but she wanted her to know the door was open if she did.

Rose flopped down on her bed and decided to call Mackenzie again. She couldn't leave it up to Grace, knowing she had Daniel and Alexis to deal with. Someone had to warn their youngest sister about her husband.

Typing in the new number she gave them, Rose waited as the phone rang. After several rings, a generic greeting came on. Rose hung up and sent her a text.

ROSE: I know you're pissed, but I really need you to call me or Gigi. It's important.

Rose sat waiting, staring at the phone for a few seconds to see if she would respond. The message remained marked as *delivered.*

CHAPTER NINE

Leslie tapped decline once again, ignoring Grace's call. She really didn't have much to say to her and wasn't quite ready to extend any forgiveness. Even though she hit Grace first, Grace was out of line for saying those things about her. She didn't have the emotional spoons to deal with her right now. Besides, now that Alexis knew the truth, she was trying to stay as far from that situation as possible. Tucking the phone back in her pocket, she glanced around the room.

"It's starting to grow on you, isn't it?" her uncle Eli asked.

Leslie smiled. "Yeah, it really is," she said, taking the space in. This was the third day she'd been here. It was like a flame, and she was the moth—drawn to it as the ideas flowed effortlessly through her. "I'm excited about all of the possibilities."

Eli nodded. "I can see that."

Leslie's beamed.

He smiled at his niece's excitement. He couldn't recall the last time he'd seen her this elated about anything, and it looked good on her. Leslie had always been the one to put everyone else's needs before her own, and now she finally had something of her own. He knew his nieces were divided about keeping it, but his gut told him that Leslie would have this place running full steam in no time.

Months ago, his brother had come to him and told him he had wanted to tell Alexis the truth. Elijah didn't know if it was guilt eating away at Ernest or the fact they'd been working on this place, and he simply wanted to clear the air before they embarked on this new endeavor.

He understood how regret could be the catalyst for a person to want to make things right. The older they got, the more time they had to reflect on their lives. However, despite his brother's desire to clear his conscience, Eli had advised him to speak to Grace first before opening that door.

"I'm thinking about swapping out the windows in here and adding more so the space is brighter and feels bigger," Leslie told him, waving her hand across the windows in front of him. "What do you think?"

"I think that's a great idea. What about the color scheme? Have you all thought about that?"

Right as she was about to answer, her phone rang again. Leslie pulled it out to see it was Grace again. She stared at it for a few seconds, groaned, then hit decline. Eli caught a glimpse and saw it was Grace calling before she ended the call.

"Have you talked to your sisters about your ideas?" he asked.

Eli watched the light fade from her eyes. He could see they were still not on the same page about keeping it, and Leslie didn't want to put a damper on her joy by bringing it up again.

"You know, I think they would get on board if you told them what you've shared with me," he encouraged.

Leslie shrugged. She'd wrestled back and forth about having a conversation with them again. Rose was onboard, but that was one person. Now with Alexis finally finding out the truth, a family project might be off the table for a while. She needed to figure out how to circumvent them and get this done. Otherwise, this place would just be sitting here, unused, and her dream would probably fizzle.

"I don't know about that, Uncle Eli. There's a lot going on right now…"

"Family will always be complicated; that doesn't mean you stop trying," he advised. "Do you think me and my siblings always got along? No, we didn't. But those are my brothers, and regardless of how mad they made me, they're my family."

Leslie listened to her uncle. Grace got under her skin in more ways than she cared to think about, but she couldn't conjure up anything that would make her cut her off altogether.

"I understand, Uncle Eli; I just think it's not a great time right now."

"And why not?"

She sighed deeply. "Lexi found out about Gigi," she admitted.

"I'm not surprised. After the way you and your sister were into it, I knew it'd come out sooner rather than later. Well, now that it's out, we can heal and move on," he said.

Leslie was a little taken back by his nonchalant response but then realized he'd probably known all along. Seeing her father and uncle were so close, her father probably didn't keep anything from him.

"I don't know if we're going to come back from this. Lexi is pretty upset."

The conversation she had with Alexis the other day was still unsettling. She could hear the pain in her voice—the anger—the resentment she now harbored toward them. Leslie had played this scenario over in her head for over a decade, trying to picture how this wouldn't be a disaster, but she always came up short.

"You will Lexi just needs time to process all of this. All of you do, especially her and Grace. It won't be overnight, but things will fall into place over time."

Leslie grinned at her uncle's optimism, hoping to God he was right.

"Come here," Eli pulled her to him, squeezing her tight. "Sometimes things have to fall apart to be put back together."

Hearing those words, feeling the sense of comfort his embrace gave her, reminded her of how much she missed her father—how neglected she felt by her husband. She didn't try to stop her tears. It'd been so long since she felt heard or even cared for.

Eli gently patted her on the back. "I'm going to get out of here, I have some other errands I need to run before it gets too late, but don't worry. Life has a way of working itself out."

Leslie hugged her uncle tightly. She needed this hug and his assurance more than he knew. Her head rested on his chest as she exhaled all the tension trapped in her body.

"How long are you going to be here?" he asked, still embracing her.

Leslie shrugged. "I don't know. I may stay a little longer and look around. I want to get a feel for the space so that when I go home. I can put some more decor boards together."

Eli smiled, impressed by her initiative.

Lifting her head, she said, "Uncle Eli, I need to ask you something, and I don't want you to think I'm trying to make you choose sides, but it'd be very remiss of me if I didn't at least inquire."

He released her and took a step back.

"What is it?"

"Is there any way I can do this without them?" Leslie gazed into his eyes. She wasn't trying to backdoor her sisters or cut them out, but she also didn't want to miss out on an opportunity because it didn't fit into their lives. Maybe this was meant for just her to do. Perhaps, this was *her* new beginning.

"Your father wanted all of you in on this, but if you can get your sisters to either sell you their percentage or sign it over to you completely, then it'll be all yours."

Getting Mackenzie and maybe even Rose to relinquish their portions probably wouldn't be difficult since Rose only caved because she begged, and Mackenzie wanted no part of it. Grace and Alexis would be something different altogether. Leslie inhaled deeply, realizing the challenge set before her, but she didn't care, she wanted this…she needed this. She was desperate for her independence.

"You make it sound so easy," she teased, slightly grinning.

"I mean, the decision is split unevenly, so it shouldn't be too hard to get them to turn it over to you."

"Yeah, right, when has anything been easy with them?"

"Good point," he chuckled. "How about this, have someone come out and appraise the property—find out how much it's worth before any more improvements—then have a conversation with them. Worst comes to worst; they'll see they probably won't get much from it, and hand it over to you."

"Good idea, Uncle Eli."

His advice was solid, and even though she wasn't completely convinced it'd be that easy, she'd at least consider it. She would also buckle down and get her business proposal done so that even if they decided not to relinquish their portions, they could see the potential and get on board with it.

"I know," he said, confidently before he leaned forward and kissed her on the forehead. I'm gonna get out of here now, don't stay too late."

"I won't promise."

He winked at her and then started walking toward the door. "And remember what I said—" he held his arm out, pointing—- "Family situations will always be complicated, but don't ever stop trying. See you later."

Leslie waved as he exited, closing the door behind him. Slowly turning in a circle, gazing at the space around her, she felt hopeful.

CHAPTER TEN

Mackenzie lowered herself in the seat, trying to remain out of sight. Her face was partially hidden behind a baseball cap she swiped from Leslie's closet before making her getaway. She was on the run, but this time with just a little more than what she arrived with. She'd left Leslie a note saying she was gone, and she'd call when she arrived at her destination.

Upon returning to her father's truck, she had Carter take her into town. He asked why one of her sisters couldn't do it, and she brushed his inquiry off with a vague response she didn't care to get into. To give the appearance, she left town, spent the night in a hotel, and left out first thing this morning; taking an Uber to the bus station before too many people woke up. She didn't want anyone to witness her exit.

Time was of the essence.

She had to get away from her parents' house, better yet, out of Deridder altogether. The last thing she wanted was for her drama to show up on her parents' doorstep though it seemed it already had. Hearing that Jasper had gone as far as to report her missing left her on edge.

"Ladies and gentlemen, we will be departing shortly. It should be about another fifteen minutes," the bus driver announced.

Fifteen minutes...fifteen minutes!

He continued. "If you need to make a restroom run, now is the time."

Mackenzie strummed her forehead as her thoughts raced. The longer they sat here, the greater her chances of being caught were. She knew if Jasper was in town, he would check all transportation locations first. Renting a car was also out since she couldn't use any of her credit cards. Mackenzie initially considered catching a flight, but then she remembered she had a duffel full of cash she couldn't exactly tote through TSA without raising some red flags.

Then there was the whole missing person's report he filed. In true Jasper fashion, he had screwed her royally.

All that was left was the bus since she could purchase a ticket with cash and bypass the extra security. Deridder wasn't a major town, so they rarely had to deal with the extra stuff most major cities encompassed.

Mackenzie rubbed her hand over her stomach to soothe the nausea. At first, she thought it was all those scents Leslie had burning at once, but then when she ordered food last night, the first whiff of it had her running to the bathroom.

Reaching for the bag her clothes were stuffed in, she grabbed the ginger ale she bought inside the station. It was one of the only things that helped settle her stomach. That was one of the upsides to Leslie knowing she was pregnant. She gave her all the pointers to combat morning sickness. Mackenzie took a few sips and put the top back on. She'd quickly learned this baby that was growing inside of her preferred small sips and bites. Too much at a time was met with regurgitation.

Mackenzie glanced down at her watch. Fifteen minutes had to be up by now. She wanted to put some distance between her and this place. Staring out of the window, Mackenzie sighed.

Love had really blinded her. Or perhaps, it was the idea of love that had her in a bind. Over the past few days, Mackenzie had a lot of time to think about her decisions regarding men. Then there was the broad conversation she had with Leslie.

People piled onto the bus one-by-one. Mackenzie casually glanced at each one of them to make sure he hadn't found her. She was certain he was on her trail. The bus filled up more than she had expected. On her trip here, it was only partially full. She figured maybe it was the time of day she traveled. It appeared more people traveled during the day, which she thought it'd be the opposite on the bus. If her trip was going to be doubled, she'd rather ride at night, that way she could sleep the majority of it.

In retrospect, she probably should've left last night, but this morning was the earliest she could get a ticket out of here. Glancing down at her watch again, Mackenzie saw fifteen minutes had passed. She tapped her knee with her fingers, silently counting down.

"Is someone sitting here?" A man asked.

"No." Mackenzie shook her head and moved her bag onto her lap.

She had hoped she would have her row to herself, but the more people that got on, the more she realized that wasn't going to happen. As the man sat down next to her, Mackenzie got a whiff of his cologne. She tilted her head toward the window, relishing the smell of bergamot cypress, sage, and cedarwood. Mackenzie could recognize that scent from anywhere. Jasper loved it and kept a bottle of it in his collection.

"Thanks, I appreciate it," he said, getting situated in his seat. "I'm not too fond of sitting in the front.

Dear God, not another one, she thought.
Mackenzie smiled, nodding. She prayed he wasn't
the chatty type because she wasn't up for much
conversation. The old woman she sat next to on the
way here literally talked her ear off. However, she
didn't mind as much since her conversation was
fairly comforting. Still, all she wanted to do now
was ride these two hours in peace.

Her phone vibrated, and she jumped.

The man gazed at her with a confused look
on his face. She didn't mean to jump, but her phone
startled her. Mackenzie fumbled inside her bag until
she located it. She hadn't programmed any numbers
since she probably wouldn't be keeping this phone
long, but she knew her mother's number by heart.
Staring at the phone, Mackenzie debated whether
she should answer it or not.

She was sure by now her sisters had told her
mother what the sheriff had told them, which was
another reason she opted out of staying at her
parents' last night. Mackenzie didn't feel like
getting the third degree about decisions she made—

poor or not. She wouldn't be able to avoid answering her mother's questions like she had Grace and Rose.

"Must be someone you don't want to talk to," the man pointed out.

Mackenzie furrowed her brow as she peered over at him. His nosiness was a bit much, considering he had sat down five minutes ago. But he was right. The phone was still vibrating in her hand. She knew she should probably let her mother know she was okay, but she wasn't ready to talk to her. Mackenzie held the phone as it rang until it stopped.

She gave it a few minutes since she knew her mother was probably going to leave a message. Although no one really left voicemails these days, her parents were still among the group of people who did. As expected, her phone buzzed and a notification that she had a voicemail appeared.

Mackenzie tapped the side of her phone, took a deep breath, and swiped the notification. She heard the doors beginning to close as she held the phone to her ear. A slight flow of relief passed through her at the creaking sound before they shut completely. *Thank God,* she prayed silently before returning to her phone. Her nerves were on edge with each minute they sat there.

She pulled the phone away from her ear when she didn't hear anything and realized she had swiped to open the message, but she didn't hit the play button. Pressing the button, she listened.

"Mackenzie Rae, I know you see me calling you, just like you saw me calling you the other day. Don't make me get in my car and drive over to your sister's house because I know that's where you are since you haven't lived here in forever and probably don't talk to anyone you went to school with. So," her mother said, pausing as if she were getting her thoughts together, *"If you do not call me back within the hour, we're going to have a problem. Especially since I found out you're married!"*

Click.

Mackenzie sat frozen with the phone still pressed against her ear. This was not how she intended for her to find out she was married. She closed her eyes at the same time she exhaled a disgruntled breath from her lips. Why wasn't she surprised that her sisters ran and told her mother her business? The least they could've done was let her do it.

She felt the bus started to move and looked up to see they were slowly drifting away from the bus station. Mackenzie tapped her text icon and decided to send them both a text. There wasn't much she had to say to them right now, but she wanted to express her displeasure with them ratting her out. Selecting their names, she added them both to the thread and started typing.

Mackenzie: *Y'all could've let me tell Mama my business instead of running to tell her.*

Mackenzie watched as the gray bubble flickered while they typed their response. Seconds later, a message came through.

Gigi: *First of all, we didn't tell her anything... your husband showed up!! And Mickey,* *how are we supposed to tell you anything when you haven't been answering your phone? You've obviously seen that we've called you, but you don't pick up or call back, so don't get pissed about something you could've avoided.*

Mackenzie's chest tightened. Her body suddenly felt flustered, and the knot in the middle of her chest had come back with a vengeance. It might've been heartburn or the fact she was a complete wreck. She bounced her leg nervously as her foot rapidly tapped the floor. Then out of nowhere, the bus pressed down hard on the brakes, stopping. Mackenzie anxiously peeked over the seat to see what was going on.

She swiped Grace's name on her phone and waited for her to pick up.

"What?" Grace shouted in her ear.

Mackenzie held the phone close to her mouth. "When did he come by?"

"Oh, now you call me," Grace answered sarcastically. "He came by the other day. Imagine my surprise to find out the sheriff wasn't lying about you being married."

Mackenzie's eyes rolled up to the ceiling. Grace and the high horse she sat on were annoying as hell. She was the last person to judge anyone right now, but Mackenzie didn't have time to lecture her on her hypocrisy. She needed to know as many details as she could get.

"Can you set aside your sarcasm for five minutes and tell me what he said?"

Grace reiterated what was said and then asked, "Are you in danger, Mickey?"

Mackenzie sighed. She'd been trying to keep her family out of her problems, but it seemed impossible at this point. She hadn't wanted to tell anyone due to the embarrassment she felt. She wasn't raised like this. Her father had never put his hands on her mother. He'd been an exemplary example of what a husband should be, so she had no excuse as to why she was allowing this. Mackenzie turned and cowered in her seat so no one would hear her.

"Yes," she murmured. "Jasper is dangerous, and you need to be leery of him."

"Dangerous, how?" Grace inquired.

"He's been hitting me for the past couple of years."

Grace gasped. She was speechless…for once. She didn't expect any of her sisters, especially Mackenzie, to be with someone who abused them. She'd always been a spitfire. Grace remembered how Rose always filled her in on Mackenzie's tussles around town. To hear this was gut-wrenching.

"I'm sorry," Grace said softly. "I didn't know."

Mackenzie wiped her eye. "I appreciate that. Now I need to know if he said he was staying or anything?"

Right at the moment Grace was about to respond, Mackenzie heard the doors open again.

"Sorry folks, it seems we have a last-minute passenger," the driver announced.

"Gigi, I need to go. I'll call you later," she told her.

Grace asked again, "Mickey, where are you?"

Her question went in one ear and out the other. Her focus was on the front of the bus. She hadn't prayed much these past few years because of everything, but at this very moment, she hoped God hadn't forgotten about her.

"I'll call you later," she repeated, then hung up.

She saw the bus driver's head turn as if someone was standing there. Mackenzie felt her heart slowly sink to the pit of her stomach. She was on pins and needles. Her body temperature rose, and the uneasiness she'd tried to ignore heightened. She took several loud, deep breaths, but nothing helped to calm her down. Grace telling her Jasper was in Deridder had her ready to make a run for it. Mackenzie looked around, searching for another exit in case she had to flee.

"Are you okay?" the man next to her asked. She was unraveling by the minute. "You don't look too well."

She wasn't well, and she was doing her best not to hyperventilate. Mackenzie fanned herself, and when that didn't help, she pulled the pamphlet her ticket was in out of her bag to fan herself with. Swallowing several times, she tried to subside the nausea she felt creeping up.

"I'm fine," she lied. "I guess I got hot all of a sudden."

He flashed her a precarious look as he examined her. She wasn't sure if he believed her and to be honest, she didn't care. Her only concern was who was getting on this bus. She caught a glimpse of a reflection on the windshield while trying to keep it hidden. When the person stepped up, she ducked down in her seat.

"Miss, are you sure you're okay?"

Mackenzie turned her head slightly. "Yes, I'm fine," she snapped.

"Okay," he held up his hand. "But you don't look fine."

Mackenzie sighed. Was she that obvious? She covered her face with her palms. Is this the kind of life she had to look forward to? Life on the run—hopping from one city to the next—constantly looking over her shoulders for the rest of her life? With a baby in tow?

None of that sounded like something she wanted to do. But she couldn't stay with Jasper and under no circumstances would he allow her to keep his money.

"I'm fine," she reiterated.

Mackenzie gradually raised her head to peek over the seat in front of her. She couldn't see much with her hat pulled down low, so she adjusted it. She squinted, trying to figure out who was up front. Once she got a better look at him, she could see it wasn't Jasper. The passenger made his way toward the back after showing the driver his ticket. As soon as he took his seat, the bus started moving again.

Mackenzie breathed heavily, pulling the cap further down over her face, then leaning the back of her head against the seat. She felt herself sinking further into her seat as she tried to disappear. Jasper had gotten too close, and the quicker she got away from here, the better.

CHAPTER ELEVEN

"Mmm, that was delicious," Daniel said, wiping his mouth. "I'll have to say this is the one thing I love most about living here—the seafood."

Grace smiled, sipping her wine. They'd made it through dinner, a couple of glasses of wine, and some rather pleasant conversation. A part of her was stalling, despite her timeline to tell him closing in as every minute passed. Since it came to light, she tried to find the right moment to drop this bomb on him, but with every opening, she thought he'd given her, she chickened out.

Now that dinner was over, the clock was ticking. It was now or never.

"Yes, it is actually really good down here. I've consumed more crawfish in the past couple of weeks than I can even recall." She laughed. "Food is definitely different in various parts of the country."

"I'm reminded of that every time I travel outside of New Orleans," he added.

Grace nodded. "It's been a minute since I've been to New Orleans. Although every time I come, I find myself eating more than I should. Drinking, too. Which is probably why I steer clear of it."

"Well, you know, you can always come to visit me." Daniel's lips formed a winsome smile as he picked up his glass. "I'm an excellent host and, surprisingly, a good tour guide. That is if there are any places left you haven't quite discovered. I'm sure, being a photographer, you've seen quite a bit of the city."

"I won't deny that," she agreed, not overlooking the open invitation he'd extended. She would gladly take him up on it if it still remained after the truth came to light. "But as far as your invitation, I'll be sure to look you up next time I'm in town."

He winked. "I'll be looking forward to that."

Grace picked up her glass and swallowed the rest of the wine. She was trying to combat her nervous energy, but nothing was working. Waving the waiter over, she held up her glass, signaling she'd like another.

"Somebody's enjoying the wine," Daniel pointed out. "That's your third glass. Are you going to be able to drive yourself home, young lady?"

Grace chuckled. "I'm fully capable of driving myself home, Daniel. It's only wine."

"Yes, but it's your third glass, and by my count, you've already consumed enough to probably cut it close to maybe…just barely—" he pinched his fingers together— "pass a breathalyzer."

"Your concern is admirable, but I'm a big girl."

"If you say so," he conceded.

The waiter returned with a glass of wine, and Grace immediately took a sip. Daniel stared at her, wondering why she suddenly seemed more fidgety, and nervous. He'd noticed it periodically during dinner; the way she kept looking off into the distance; the constant tapping of her finger as if she was thinking about something; but mostly how she looked like there was something lingering at the tip of her tongue.

"I promise I'll be fine. If it comes down to it, I'll call an Uber," she told him. "I know when I'm incapable of driving."

"That's a relief. However, I'm curious as to what have you so nervous. Is it me?"

If you only knew. Grace huffed silently. She was nervous, terrified, uncertain…all of the above, but mostly worried. Worried that he wouldn't understand her reason behind what occurred. Grace circled the rim of her glass, figuring she'd held out long enough.

"Daniel, I have something to tell you. And before I do, I want you to know none of this was intentional." Grace looked away for a second, then back at him. "I didn't have much of a choice, and I need you to know that."

"Grace, what's going on?" Daniel leaned forward with an uneasy look on his face.

Taking another long sip, she replied, "It's about our child, the one we allegedly gave up for adoption."

His brow lifted slightly, but enough to where she could tell he'd heard every word she said and piqued his interest. He stared at her attentively, waiting for her to finish.

"I haven't been exactly honest about what transpired, and now, due to recent events, it's time for me to tell you the whole truth."

"Grace, I don't understand. You're speaking in riddles. Did something happen to her? Has someone contacted you? What's going on?"

"Yes and no. Thirty-one years ago, we agreed to give our daughter up for adoption—and I did—but the people who adopted her were my parents." Grace exhaled before continuing. "Daniel, Alexis is our daughter. As in my sister Alexis."

The playfulness that was once in his eyes faded, quickly replaced with bewilderment and fury. His jaw clenched while his mouth formed into a tightlipped frown. He'd forfeited knowing any details regarding her identity to help him cope with what they'd done, including her name. He never asked her what she named their daughter because he'd given up the right to know.

The only thing he'd programmed to memory was her birthdate—July 15, 1989. It's been embedded into the deepest corners of his mind. Right next to Sydney's birthday. To hear that she'd spent every single birthday with her when they agreed to give her up for adoption, he was furious.

The awkward silence hovering over them started to feel uncomfortable. Grace searched his face for something, anything that would give her some clue as to what was going through his mind, but she came up empty.

"Let me get this straight; you're telling me that *your sister* is, in fact, *our daughter?* The daughter we agreed to give up for adoption; the child you told me we had to sign our rights over for; the child—" he spoke through gritted teeth— "the child who's been living right under my nose all this time and you never once said a thing!"

His voice increased a few octaves, causing people at the neighboring tables to glance over at them. Grace's breathing sped up, matching the tempo of her heartbeat and her heightened nerves. She tried to shield her face from the embarrassment she felt. This was why she didn't want to do this in public, but with him leaving and them being in a public place, she somewhat felt he might keep his cool and not make a scene.

"Daniel, before you overreact—"

"Overreact…overreact…are you kidding me right now, Grace? You drop something like this on me and think I won't be upset about it. *Overreact?* For thirty-something-years, you've been lying to me—*lying*!"

"I know, but I need you to give me a chance to explain," she whispered. "Can you please calm down so I can do so?"

"Don't tell me to calm down. You don't get to do that right now. I can't believe you've been harboring this secret all this time."

"If you just let me I—"

"No!" He pounded his fist on the table. The silverware rattled against the porcelain as the table shook. The tone and the volume of his voice echoed. Grace wanted to get up and leave but knew she had to finish telling him everything. Alexis blindsiding him would only make this worse. "You don't get to make demands here."

The waiter returned. "I'm sorry, is everything okay?" he asked.

Grace forced a smile onto her lips. "Yes, everything is fine. Could you bring us the check, please?"

"Sure, I have it right here," he replied, retrieving the billfold from his apron. Quickly shuffling through the receipts, he located theirs and sat it down on the table. "I'll be back whenever you're ready."

Daniel instantly picked it up, gazed at it, and pulled his wallet out. "Here—" he opened his wallet, counting out the bills. Then he placed two-hundred-dollar bills on the table— "Keep the change."

"Thank you," the waiter said, wasting no time scurrying off.

Horror knotted Grace's stomach when Daniel stood. "Daniel, we're not finished."

"I am," he said, turning to leave.

Rushing behind him, she ignored all the weird stares directed at her. She knew once he got into his car; he would drive off without another word.

"Daniel, please…wait!"

"I don't have anything to say to you right now, Grace!"

"I can explain why if you just give me a chance."

With all the shouting, they managed to make it across the parking lot and to his car. Stopping in his tracks, he turned around and glared at her. Grace stopped, too, making sure to leave enough space between them.

"Hear me out, please," she pleaded. "I know it seems like I misled you, but that's not the case at all."

"Misled? Misled? Do you think that's all that you did? Grace, you flat-out lied to me! You deceived me into believing the child we created was out in the world, somewhere with God knows who, when all this time she was living in your house!"

Grace's breaths were uneven. "I do not disagree with you. I'm only asking that you see this from my perspective. At least let me tell you why things transpired the way they did."

He scoffed. "Your perspective? For years, I beat myself up about that decision. I lived with this hole in my heart after reading your Dear John letter, never to hear from you again. It took what seemed like forever for me to set aside the feelings of guilt and doubt. Maybe she didn't think I'd be a good father. Perhaps she didn't want a child with me. Did she or did she not want to be a mother? These are the questions and thoughts I battled with for years, Grace. Don't you see how this one lie created so much turmoil in my life? Now you want to wipe the slate clean by explaining your treachery," he scolded.

Grace shrunk inside of herself. With each word he spewed, she felt smaller and smaller. His reaction was warranted, expected even. Still, she thought he'd be a little more levelheaded. At least, she hoped he would. She was speechless. Unsure of what to say next since it seemed whatever she did say only made him madder.

"Why now?" he asked, interrupting her pity party. "What prompted this confession? You've gone this long without feeling the need to confide in me."

"Because something happened, and I felt you needed to know," she answered truthfully. Sighing, Grace locked eyes with him. "Alexis…she found out and more or less demanded to know who you were."

"Found out?" He snickered sinisterly. "Found out how?"

"Is that important? She knows and wants to know how you are, so instead of letting her blindside you, I'm telling you."

"Typical Grace. Always giving just enough, yet never everything. You tell me something of this magnitude, then have the audacity to decipher what's not important—how do you fathom that's okay? I asked you how she found out."

"Me. She overheard me talking to my mother about it. My father wrote me a letter and put it in my bag the last time I visited. I never bothered to open it until I was headed back here for his funeral. He wanted me to know he was sorry for the position they put me in, the secrets that were kept, everything. He also wanted me to tell Alexis the truth, which was my takeaway. Anyhow, I was on the fence about it and mentioned it to my mother. I didn't know Alexis was behind me."

Daniel shook his head. "In other words, you didn't have any intention of saying anything; it came out by mistake," he asked and answered.

"Daniel..."

"No, stop. I don't want to hear anything else," he turned around to open his door, "Nothing you can say will make this alright, Grace...nothing. It's unforgivable."

Grace held her tongue as she watched him climb into his car and start the ignition. The word *unforgivable* reverberated throughout her, leaving her to question if this would be the same outcome when she finally spoke to Alexis. Daniel peered over at her one last time before he drove off and left her standing there.

CHAPTER TWELVE

Alexis held the box in her hand, staring at it as she read the instructions. Her search for her place of birth had come up empty thus far. She'd gone over the conversation she had with Leslie. At least she had a name…that was a start. Now she needed to locate him.

"Ugh," she pouted, tossing the box on the coffee table. "What is this really going to do? I just wasted my money."

She stared at the box with *AncestryDNA* in bold letters across the front of it. Alexis had no idea how doing this would help, but she was hoping it'd give her some idea of whether he lived close to her or across the country like Grace.

"What are the chances he still lives in Deridder?" she asked herself, tossing the box on the table.

Her phone screen lit up.

Alexis peered over to glance at it. *Her mother.* She was calling again. She wanted to ask her about Daniel, but she couldn't since she promised Leslie that she wouldn't oust her for telling her.

Knowing she'd only keep calling, Alexis picked up her phone. "Hello?" she answered.

"Lexi! Where are you?" her mother asked.

"I'm at home."

Her mother grunted in her ear. "When were you going to let me know that you made it home? You left here like a mad woman, headed to God knows where, and didn't say anything. A simple— Mom, I made it home would've been nice."

Alexis bit down on her tongue, choosing to exhale her frustrations instead. Although she was upset at her mother, she knew disrespecting her wasn't an option either. The last thing she needed was for her to show up at her door, nor did she need the goon squad calling to scold her.

"I'm sorry, I didn't really feel like talking to anyone after everything that happened."

"That's understandable, but no one knew where you'd gone or anything," her mother told her. "You could've been on the side of the road for all I knew."

Leslie knew, she thought, but decided to leave that tidbit out as well since she knew the moment she said it, her mother would be calling Leslie to give her a piece of her mind, too.

"I just needed some time… still do, if I'm being honest. All of this, it's just a lot." Alexis leaned back and gazed up at the ceiling. "Why didn't you tell me? I asked you at the house, and you told me you were leaving it up to Gigi, but was that the real reason?"

There was a long pause as her mother collected her thoughts. Regardless of what she said, there was nothing she could think of that would possibly make up for the years of lies and deceit.

"Honestly, Lexi, there never seemed to be a good time to tell you. I thought about telling you when you graduated high school and again when you moved out, but the words kept getting stuck. I

161

figured we'd gone all this time, so what would be the point? Then your father decided to write Gigi that letter and I thought—well, he's right—Gigi should tell her."

"But you knew she wouldn't."

"I didn't. After your father expressed his feelings and apologized to her, I thought it would be the nudge she needed to reconcile with everything and maybe finally tell you."

Alexis shook her head. Everyone knew Grace was stubborn, and regardless of how much she was nudged, if she didn't want to do it—she wouldn't. The two of them passing the torch to her was simply their way of absolving themselves of the responsibility. Her mother admitting that only confirmed it.

"What I don't understand is why you won't tell me who he is. It serves no point in keeping it a secret now," Alexis told her. Even though she knew the truth, some of it anyway, she still wasn't letting her mother off the hook. She was complicit in this lie and continued to be by not being more forthcoming. "Why is everyone protecting him?"

"No one is protecting him, Lexi."

"Yes, you are!"

"Alexis Bayou, I understand you're upset, but that doesn't mean I'm going to allow you to yell at me. I raised you, and you will speak to me with respect."

Alexis said nothing as they listened to each other breathe. She was fuming, and there were so many things she wanted to say, but none of them would come out respectfully or calmly. She realized her mother wasn't going to budge on her decision and saw no point in continuing this conversation. She had a name, and that was enough to start with.

"I need to go. I'll call you later," she said.

"Lexi…"

"I'll call you later, Ma."

"Alright," her mother said, hanging up.

As she tossed the phone down next to her, Alexis's eyes watered at how naive she'd been. People always said she and Grace favored each other, but she never thought anything about because they were sisters. But here they were, a couple of decades later, and the revelation of her parentage had completely blindsided her.

Alexis wiped her cheeks. Her eyes landed on the box again. Questions raced through her mind.

Does she really want to get to know complete strangers?

Does her real father's family live nearby?

Does he?

Does she have siblings?

Is she his only child?

She knew she was as far as Grace was concerned. But he was a different story altogether.

One thought after the other ran through her mind. She'd gone this long without knowing him or them. Did she really want to know? What if they were completely opposite of the family she had? Would they be better or worse? Do they know about her? Or was she a secret to everyone?

Has her father thought about her after all these years?

The mere fact her biological father happily walked away left her wondering if he really wanted her or whether he was happy to bow out and be rid of his responsibilities like Grace.

Grace. She exhaled and then scowled at the thought of her.

Grace's reluctance to reveal her paternity only fueled her disgust.

Alexis massaged her pressure points on both sides of her head just as she heard jiggling at her door. Sitting up straight, she stared at her doorknob. Over and over, someone jiggled it while trying to unlock her door.

"Oh, hell no," she mumbled, hopping up to grab her gun out of the table next to her.

She wasn't a fan of firearms, but her father bought her one after learning she was working all of those crazy pandemic shifts. He already felt some kind of way about her living alone with no weapon, but finding out she was working graveyard shifts—he sprung into protective mode. She'd only shot it a few times at the range and wasn't exactly a sniper, but she could hit her mark if need be.

Removing the safety, she pointed her weapon at the door. "Whoever is at my door, I promise you, you do not want to open it. Step away from it and go back to where you came from," she warned.

Alexis cuffed the grip tighter as she waited for their next move. She was ready for whatever if that meant she'd have to shoot someone. She didn't want to, but she had no intention of becoming a victim of any kind. Inhaling deeply, she expelled soft breaths. Her heart was racing. Even the hair on the back of her neck was standing. Her mouth was suddenly super wet.

Taking one step at a time, Alexis moved toward her window. Gun still aimed at the door; she slowly pushed the curtains back so she could look out of the window. There was no car parked in her driveway, so who was at her door?

Closing the curtain, Alexis eased toward her phone. She'd at least call the police that way there'd be something on file she was defending herself. The handle shook repeatedly as she picked up her phone.

By the sound of it, they were still fumbling with the lock. She took her key from Keith and changed her locks; therefore, no one else had a key to her house. Alexis' eyes roamed back and forth. Did he make a copy?

"This is your last warning. Get the hell away from my door," she shouted, unlocking her phone.

"Lexi, open the damn door!"

Alexis rolled her eyes at the same time she lowered her gun. Walking over to the door, she peeked through the peephole and saw it was Mackenzie. Unlocking it, she peered through the chain.

"What are you doing here, Mickey? And why didn't you call?"

"Why are you talking to me through the door crack? Open the door!" Mackenzie commanded, pushing on the door.

Alexis shut the door, slid the chain back, and opened it to her sister bouncing up and down like a toddler. She quirked a brow at how juvenile she looked.

"Why are you bouncing like a four-year-old?" she asked, stepping back.

Mackenzie shoved her way inside. "If you must know, I need to pee. That ginger ale I drank on the bus hit me in the Uber." She dropped her bags. Noticing the gun, she asked, "Why do you have a gun out?"

"Maybe because I thought someone was breaking into my house." She put the gun on the table next to her.

"Mmm hmm, aren't you the person who just lectured Uncle Eli on guns?" she teased.

"Why are you here, Mickey?" she rolled her eyes.

"We'll get to that." Looking around, she said, "You redecorated. I need to use the bathroom."

Not giving her a chance to say anything else, Mackenzie darted off to the restroom. She knew Alexis was going to interrogate her, so she'd at least empty her bladder first.

"When you get done, you're going to tell me why you're here," Alexis shouted, moving Mackenzie's bags to the side so she wouldn't trip over them.

Since she was up, she figured she'd pour herself a glass of wine. Another addiction or possibly suppressant of hers these days. If she wasn't drowning her numbness in wine, it was Keith. Alexis filled her goblet up midway and walked back to where she was seated. Plopping down on the couch, she waited for her sister to join her.

Seconds passed before she heard the toilet flush and the faucet turn on. Afterward, the hallway lit up momentarily, and Mackenzie reappeared. Alexis peered over her shoulder as she sipped her wine. Plopping down next to Alexis, Mackenzie kicked her feet up, then leaned her head against the back of the couch.

Alexis peered over at her. "I'm ready to hear why you randomly popped up at my house, considering you didn't bother giving me any notice. And does anyone know you're here?"

"My fault. I wasn't counting on you being here."

The audacity her baby sister displayed sometimes threw her for a loop.

"You didn't expect me to be at *my house*? Where else would I be? Who shows up to someone's house not expecting them to be there?"

Mackenzie sighed.

"Exactly," Alexis continued. "It didn't even make sense to you when you said it."

Mackenzie lifted her legs on the ottoman, trying to get situated on the couch before she gathered her sister. "I didn't know where you would be because, like I said, you're not responding. I would've at least thought you'd tell me where you were, but when you didn't; I figured you were hiding out somewhere."

"I'm not you, Mickey. I don't hide from the world. And even if that were the case, it still doesn't explain why you're here?"

"I needed a change of scenery," Mackenzie lied.

Alexis took another sip of wine. She knew there was more to this story. Mackenzie stared at the inviting beverage she couldn't have, and a pinch of sadness swept over her. In her condition, she wouldn't taste a drop of alcohol for another year.

"Do you have to drink that in front of me?"

Alexis craned her neck back. "I know you didn't show up at my house—unannounced—and want to tell me what I can or cannot drink. You couldn't be doing that."

Mackenzie huffed her eyes and hopped up to get something to drink.

"No one told you to get knocked up," Alexis teased.

"Whatever. What else do you have to drink that isn't going to put me into early labor?" she asked, opening the refrigerator.

"There's water," Alexis replied.

"Whatever, Lexi. You don't have any tea or anything?"

"I haven't gone shopping since I've been back. I wasn't expecting company, so again...whatever's in there."

Annoyed with her options, Mackenzie pulled the Brita pitcher out to pour herself some water. This had to be the worst time for her not to be able to drink. Reappearing, she rejoined Alexis. As she sat down, she caught a glimpse of the box on the table she'd missed when she first arrived.

Reaching for it, she asked, "Umm, what's this for?"

"Dang, Mickey, can you mind your business?" Alexis snatched the box back. "It's something I'm considering."

Mackenzie sipped her water. She didn't really need to ask why Alexis was considering that service as an option. With no one telling her what she wanted to know, she was trying other options. She just wanted her to talk to someone about it because she always had a bad habit of keeping things bottled up and then exploding.

"I tried asking Leslie who he was, but she wouldn't budge," Mackenzie told her.

Alexis chuckled. "Are you surprised?" She continued to pretend she was unaware of who her father was, like she promised.

"Do you want to talk about it?" Mackenzie inquired.

"No, I don't. I do, however, want to talk about why you're here," Alexis said, circling back around. "What happened now?"

"What makes you think something happened?

Alexis cocked her head to the side. "Fine," Mackenzie said and filled her in on all that had happened.

Alexis's eyes widened at her revelation. "In other words, they tried to force you to tell them everything, huh?"

"Girl! I was like hold up, especially with Gigi 'cause girl…you just—" Mackenzie stopped mid-sentence. "Never mind."

"It's cool, Mickey. The truth is the truth. Why she's worried about your secrets, and she has her own is a lot to process, but that's Grace for you." She raised her glass in the air.

Mackenzie could hear the animosity and contempt in Alexis' voice. It wasn't going to be an overnight miracle, but she prayed this situation would be resolved without ripping her family any further apart.

"You're going to have to talk to her eventually, Lexi."

"And you're going to have to deal with your marital issues eventually," she retorted bluntly.

"I know that, and I'm handling it."

"No, you're not, you're running, but that's your choice. What else did Sheriff Landry tell them?"

"I have no idea. I didn't get to ask your nosy sisters because they were too busy lecturing me. But whatever was said, Jasper got wind of where I was and showed up on Mama's porch."

"Mickey! Did he see you? Better yet, does he know you're here?"

"Calm down and no. I actually left not long after I got into it with Rose and Gigi. Initially, I was just going to go somewhere to cool off and come back, but then I knew they would eventually bring it up again. I didn't feel like explaining myself, so I stayed at Leslie's house."

Alexis shook her head. "Does Leslie know about him and how crazy he is?"

"No, but she does know I'm pregnant." Mackenzie chuckled. "She busted me out when I tried to act like I wasn't."

"Why wouldn't you tell her or at least Mama so they know he's a psychopath?"

"I told Gigi," Mackenzie admitted. "Mama left me a rather harsh voicemail, so I texted Gigi about snitching, and she confirmed he showed up out of the blue. I called her and ended up telling her why I ran. I'm sure Mama knows by now."

"I'm sure Grace had a lot to say."

"Surprisingly, she seemed concerned. We didn't get to finish because someone got on the bus late, and I thought it was Jasper."

"What are you going to do about Jasper?"

"I don't know." Mackenzie rubbed her forehead. "Thinking about it stresses me out. Then I get overwhelmed and push it to the back of my mind."

"How's that working out for you?" Alexis asked.

"It was fine until I called to check on my shop. Jasper walked in on Nina talking to me and went into a manic frenzy. He basically threatened me because I wouldn't tell him where I was or admit I had his money, which is when he got the bright idea to report me missing. I know it was just to draw me out, but I never expected him to walk into a police station."

Alexis glanced at her. "Why not?"

Mackenzie gazed at one of the duffel bags Alexis had placed on the bench by her closet. The contents of that bag are why she was surprised he did. Jasper didn't necessarily operate on the up-and-up. He had legit businesses, but they were fronts to funnel money. Her shop was somewhat a part of that network. She didn't wash his money, only used her shop as a drop-off location. Luckily, she was smart enough to register it under her name.

Alexis eyes followed her sister's. "Is it worth it?" Alexis asked, slicing through Mackenzie's thoughts. "The money? Is keeping it worth you having to look over your shoulder for the foreseeable future?"

Mackenzie mulled over her question. Alexis had no is what she'd endured these past few years to the point she felt she very much deserved every dollar that bag contained. It was the only way she

could start fresh, and now that she was pregnant —
she definitely needed it.

"Depends on what you consider worth it. To
me, yes, it is."

"Why? Why is keeping his money so
important? Seems like an easy fix to a major
problem to me —giving it back to him."

I wish, Mackenzie thought. That wouldn't
even begin to eliminate her problems. The stolen
money wasn't what had gotten under his skin; his
loss of control did. Narcissists hated losing control.
It was their drug, the thing that got them high.
Mackenzie disrupting that control is the real reason
he wanted to set everything ablaze.

The money was just an added bonus.

"That wouldn't even begin to fix this mess,"
she admitted.

"But it'd be a start… an olive branch,
maybe?"

Mackenzie smiled at her sister's naïveté.
She wanted to be as hopeful as Alexis was, but she

knew better. "Jasper isn't going to stop until he has the money *and* me. He feels betrayed."

"You still haven't said what you're going to do? Are you staying here? Going back to Deridder? Atlanta? What's your plan I can tell you uprooting every time you think he's found you isn't the answer either. You'll be running for the rest of your life without one."

"I don't know. I'm still figuring that part out. I just need a place to crash and gather my thoughts together. That's what I would do in Deridder, but he managed to find me."

"Mickey, you know you can stay here as long as you need, but you can't stay here forever. At some point, you're gonna have to face this because if he shows up here—in the state I'm in—I'm definitely going to shoot him."

Mackenzie huffed. "Tell me something I don't know."

"And the baby?"

"What about it?"

Alexis turned to face her. "Are you keeping it or?"

"Haven't quite figured that part out either."

"Do you want to be a mother?"

Mackenzie tossed her question around in her mind. She hadn't thought about that in a long time. In the beginning, she was elated to start a family with Jasper, but as of late, she couldn't fathom being tethered to him any more than she already was.

"Once upon a time," she answered, "Now…these days…I'm not so sure."

"I take it it's contingent upon your marital situation."

Silence settled between them for a few moments as Alexis's statement hung in the air.

"How far along are you?"

Mackenzie shrugged.

"I suggest you get to a doctor or a clinic soon, so you have a better grasp of what your options are. Otherwise, nature is going to decide for you."

"I can't," Mackenzie murmured.

"And why not?"

"I want a divorce, and the instant I hear a heartbeat, I'll know that isn't possible," she said, defeated.

Alexis scrunched her face. "I don't understand,"

"Jasper won't give me a divorce if he knows I'm pregnant."

"Then don't tell him. Problem solved."

Not really, Mackenzie told herself. He'd drag this out to the point she'd be showing.

"It's not that simple."

"I don't see why not. Find a lawyer, file the paperwork, and have him serve. The two of you go through the mediation, or whatever it's called, split your assets, and go your separate ways amicably."

Mackenzie stared at her sister. Alexis's breakdown of divorce proceedings seemed so simple, and for some, that might be the case, but for her —not likely.

Alexis placed her hand on her sister's arm. "What do you need from me? I know some great doctors at the hospital. I can get you in to see one of them," Alexis suggested, "That way, you can know if everything is okay with the baby."

Mackenzie shook her head. "I can't. I don't want any records lying around."

"I don't understand. Just pretend you don't know you're pregnant."

"I can't do that if there are records of me knowing."

"Mickey, you're not making any sense."

"Once I file, I'm going to have to disclose I'm pregnant,, which will halt the divorce. He's never going to walk away that easily. I know that. That's why I ran."

"I mean, is there a law that says you have to tell him?"

Alexis was curious since she really didn't know, but this didn't seem like an obstacle. More like a 'don't ask, don't tell' situation. Volunteering information is where the issue arises.

"In a normal situation, I would; however, because my situation involves domestic violence—I don't. But not telling him means he will have no part in my child's life."

"Isn't that what you want, though? For him to be gone for good?" Alexis questioned.

Mackenzie sighed. "This whole situation sucks. I never imagined my life or marriage would turn out like this. How did I go from being blissfully happy to hiding from the man I love? Then to make it worse, now I have to keep our child safe by keeping Jasper away from him or her."

Alexis's heart bled for her sister.

"Hmm," Alexis hummed, thinking how ironic it was that Mackenzie was in the same predicament Grace was in years ago, but worse.

"What?"

"Nothing. I guess I was thinking about how you're in the same situation Gigi was in all those years ago."

"How so?"

183

"You're going to have to keep your child's paternity a secret, too now."

Sitting up, Mackenzie glanced at her. "Umm, no, we're not. There is a vast difference between my situation and Gigi's. She had no reason to lie to you other than she wanted to. Don't get me wrong. Her situation was an unfortunate one with them making her do that; however, she could've told you later on. In my case, my safety is in jeopardy. Me keeping Jasper a secret is to protect myself and my child. Gigi was protecting herself."

Still is, Alexis told herself.

"Speaking of which, what will you do about that?" Mackenzie asked, motioning toward the box. "Are you going to take the test?"

"I'm still trying to figure that out, but I want to know. I want to know the truth. I'm just not sure how to feel about it."

The two of them sank into the plush cushions as their thoughts roamed wildly across their minds. Here Alexis was, yearning to know who her father was; meanwhile, Mackenzie was doing her best to keep her pregnancy under wraps. They were on opposite ends of the spectrum with the same problem in the middle...secrets.

CHAPTER THIRTEEN

Rose opened the door and walked in. Every nerve in her body was going off as she looked around at people moving about. The ringing phones, file cabinets opening and closing, people moving about, the smell of crappy coffee—a busy police department. Even though she wasn't in trouble, she still didn't enjoy the thought of having to be here. She gripped the strap on her bag as she prepared herself for the second hardest thing she would have to do.

Moving forward, she eased toward the front desk to inform the receptionist of her arrival so she could inform Detective Graves. The sooner she got out of here, the better. This nightmare was almost over for her, and she could start the healing journey she was desperately ready to begin.

Rose smiled at her. "Hello, my name is Rose Bayou, and I'm here to see Detective Graves."

"Hello. Do you have an appointment?" she asked.

"I do," I said with a smile.

The receptionist nodded and picked up the phone to call him. Rose waited as she repeated the information that she'd just given her. Seconds later, she hung up and gazed back at Rose. "He'll be out in just a second—" she told her, extending her hand— "you can have a seat if you'd like."

Rose peeked over to her right at the empty chairs, smiling and nodding. "Thank you," she said, then walked over to the chairs. She welcomed the idea of sitting down since her knees were already shaky. Identifying Lucien seemed like a good idea a few days ago, but now that she was here, she hated that she had agreed to it. Nothing inside of her was prepared to do this, even if he couldn't see her on the other side of that glass. She could see him.

"Miss Bayou," someone said, interrupting her thoughts.

Glancing up, Rose answered, "Yes."

"I'm glad you came in," Detective Graves replied, holding out his hand.

Rose shook it and then stood. "Didn't exactly have a choice, did I?"

"Very much so. This is an open and shut case; however, witness statements always help make sure criminals stay behind bars." He smiled and ushered her toward the back. "This should be pretty quick. I just had a few more questions to ask you, and once that's done, you'll be good to go, and all of this will be behind you."

Far from it, Rose thought as she exhaled the deep breath she'd been holding onto. With each step she took, she felt her chest tighten. She followed him as they walked toward the back, where she would be identifying the man she thought she'd be spending the rest of her life with.

"Right in here," he said, pulling out the chair.

Detective Graves sat down at his desk and pulled out the folder pertaining to her case. He flipped it open and turned it around to face her. "I

189

just need you to look over this and confirm that everything in here is correct as far as the items taken along with the money stolen."

Rose glanced down, and the first thing that caught her eye was a mugshot of Lucien. Slowly, she pushed the breath she'd been holding to prevent herself from getting choked up. There he was, holding a letterboard with his real name and his new inmate number. He looked rough and rugged, unlike his usual well-groomed self.

Detective Graves asked, "Is everything correct, Miss Bayou?"

Rose redirected her attention and focused on the documents. She skimmed over them, one-by-one, until she finished all six pages. *Six pages,* she thought. Her life with Lucien had been reduced to six pages. "Yes," she answered. "Everything is correct."

"Great," he said.

"May I have a copy of that report?" Rose asked.

He closed the folder and gazed at her. "Of course, I will get you a modified copy that we give to civilians to have for your records. You'll need them to file with your bank or anyone else for fraud purposes."

"Thank you."

"Well, Miss Bayou, that's it. Hopefully, this will offer you some sense of peace. I know it won't erase what happened to you, but at least you can find comfort in knowing that he's behind bars and can no longer do it to anyone else."

Rose nodded, giving him a partial smile. She appreciated his words of comfort, but the need to see Lucien and ask him why still lingered. She knew there was a possibility he'd probably lie, but there was a small ounce of optimism that she hoped he wouldn't. Her heart kept telling her she needed closure to move on.

"Detective, I have a favor to ask you."

Detective Graves leaned back. "Sure, what is it?"

"I wanted to ask if there was perhaps a chance that I could see him?"

Rose watched as his face became flooded with uncertainty. She knew it was a big risk, and probably prohibited, but she'd kick herself if she didn't ask. He stared at her for what felt like forever. His hesitation in granting her request was obvious. But then, he leaned forward.

"Rose…may I call you Rose?" he asked.

Rose nodded, granting him permission.

"Rose, I don't think that's a good idea. Not only that, but we don't typically allow victims to speak with perpetrators. If there is a message you would like me to relay, I can have one of the correctional officers do so."

Rose shook her head. "No, that's not good enough—" she moved closer so no one else could hear her— "I just need to face him one last time— let him see my face and ask him why he did it."

"Miss Bayou… I mean Rose. Men like Xavier Conway don't have reasons for why they do what they do. Not logical ones, anyway. I guarantee that you are better off leaving here and forgetting about him," he advised.

Rose felt the disappointment creep up. She needed to appeal to him in some other way in order for him to grant her request. Rose perused his desk, catching a glimpse of a picture of a little girl. She was adorable, and Rose wondered if that was his daughter. She pointed at it.

"Your daughter?"

His face lit up as his eyes traveled to the picture. "Yes, her name is Gabriella, but I call her Gabby for short."

Rose picked up on how proud he sounded when he answered. She glanced at the picture again and saw how much they resembled each other, then she looked back at him.

"What if it were her sitting here? Better yet, what if she came home one day and told you that something similar had happened to her? Wouldn't you want to do everything in your power to help ease her mind? I'm not asking for two hours; I'm not even asking for an hour. I just need to hear some kind of explanation from him. Even if it's a brief one."

Detective Graves thought long and hard about her request. He understood her need to speak with him. He could grasp her quest for closure after dealing with several victims and their families. However, he'd seen enough to also know seeking closure from the person who harmed you was an unrealistic trap because no matter what reason was given; it never made what they did any better. The unknown was a gift, and most people didn't understand that.

"Please," Rose uttered.

He folded his hands on his desk. "I don't think seeing him is a good idea," he stated reluctantly. "That being said, I will give you ten minutes—not a minute more—to get whatever answers you think you need." He stood up. "Follow me. I'll take you down to where you can speak with him."

Rose stood, accepting his terms. "Thank you."

Detective Graves led her to the elevators. Lucien was held a couple of floors down from where they were. The two of them walked down the long corridor to where visitors were allowed to speak to inmates. They stopped at the desk where the clerk was seated.

"Hello, Amanda," he greeted her.

"Afternoon, Detective. What can I do for you?"

"I need you to have Xavier Conway brought out of his cell, please. There's someone here to see him."

Amanda glanced at Rose as she placed the clipboard on the counter. "Sure, I just need you to sign in here," she told Rose.

Rose took a pen out of the holder and scribbled her name down. Once she finished, Amanda wrote her name on a name tag and handed it to her. Rose accepted it and stuck it on her chest.

"I'll have him brought out to station four," Amanda informed them.

"Thank you," Detective Graves said, placing his hand on the small of Rose's back to usher her to where she could speak to him.

The two of them walked down another hallway before they arrived in a dimly lit space with a row of sectioned-off areas for people to talk to inmates. Rose didn't think this was how she would be speaking to him, but she'd take what she could get.

"Station four is right over there," he pointed.

Rose nodded. "Thank you."

She pulled out the chair and sat down. On the other side were a dingy cream wall and a grey steel door she assumed he'd be walking out of. The glass had scratches and was somewhat cloudy. There was no telling how often they cleaned it, which made her cringe about putting that phone to her ear. Of all the times to forget her Clorox wipes.

Time seemed to stand still as she sat waiting for the door to open. Minutes later, Lucien appeared dressed in a pewter shirt and pants. Rose locked eyes with Lucien...or should she say, Xavier. She lifted the phone and wiped it on her lap, then held it to her ear. Lucien sat down in front of her, looking like a shell of the man she fell in love with.

"Rose," he spoke once he picked up the phone.

"Lucien, or should I call you Xavier?"

Rose searched his eyes for some kind of remorse. Why? She couldn't quite explain, except that she'd hoped he would display an ounce of regret. Lucien's lips curved into a sly grin and Rose knew there would be no apologies on his behalf.

"Was any of it real?" she asked.

Lucien leaned closer to the glass. "Some of it was, some of it wasn't."

"Why me, Lucien? Why did you do it?"

"Because you were an easy mark."

His blatant, unempathetic response forced Rose to swallow the hurt that crept up. It was cold, callous, void of the love he once told her he had for her.

"Then why did you propose? Matter of fact, why bother spending three years with me if this is how it was going to end? You could've stolen everything in a matter of months; why did you stick around all that time?" She cleared her throat, trying to rid it of the angst she felt.

"I did what I had to do. You weren't stupid, and you're far from being too trusting. I spotted this early, so I was playing the long game. But there was one thing you couldn't help but project…"

Lucien appeared equanimous. Unbothered by the hurt he inflicted on her. His blasé expressions indicated he was far from affected by his actions. Rose glared at him, realizing—once a criminal, always a criminal.

"And what was that?" she asked.

"Your desperation."

Rose sat muted. She was unable to fully process what he said because she couldn't believe he'd said it. There were a lot of characteristics and flaws she'd account for, but desperation wasn't something she'd label herself as. She'd always exhibited self-respect and possessed high self-esteem.

"I am far from desperate."

He cackled sinisterly in her ear. "You and I both know that's a lie." He scoffed. "You're like most women your age. Successful in every area of your life, accept love. So much so you'll overlook a variety of tell-tale signs to have it. Face it, you're a forty-something woman with no kids and you've never been married. You're not exactly a man's first choice. You're past your prime to have children. Your youth is long gone, so you don't exactly have that going for you. You've managed to stay in shape…thank God, but other than that—you're undesirable. It's understandable you'd take what you could get. But who's really out here rushing to marry an almost fifty-year-old woman? Nobody. Believe it or not, I did you a favor, Rose."

His words stung. How had she not seen this side of him? Regardless of how much she wanted love, she'd never compromised her standards to obtain it. Lucien was just a good con-artist, and that was the truth. She wasn't going to allow him to sit across from her and shift the blame onto her.

"You know you're right about one thing," she told him.

"And what's that?" he asked with a cocky grin plastered on his face. "What am I right about, baby?"

Rose scowled at him then she narrowed her eyes. "You're right about me missing a sign. It wasn't until now that I realized you are a selfish, narcissistic prick who I'm happy showed me who he was before I made the fatal mistake of tying myself to him. I'm glad I could see that you are a fraud who has to fake being in love with someone because the truth is…no one would really want him if they knew who you were beneath all that charm and lies. So, thank you. Thank you for wasting three years of my life instead of the rest of it." Rose scooted the chair back and stood up. "My time is up here, but I hope you enjoy prison. Meanwhile, I'll enjoy my freedom and the fruits of my labor. Please, don't write. Goodbye, Xavier."

Rose slammed the phone on the receiver and turned around to see Detective Graves.

"Rose! Rose! Get back here! I'm not done with you yet!" Xavier yelled.

Rose ignored his desperate pleas, walked over to Detective Graves, and said, "I'm ready."

"Are you sure?" he asked.

"Yes, this chapter of my life is over. He's right where she should be. Time to move on."

CHAPTER FOURTEEN

Leslie stretched out on her couch as she caught up on her television shows. She did quite a bit of work regarding the estate, setting up appointments, screening appraisers, and finishing a few designs. Now she was going to enjoy the rest of her kid-free day. The kids were with Mathias. She wasn't ready to deal with *their* situation yet. Maybe she was in denial. Or perhaps, she was over it.

She got up to refill her afternoon cocktail. As she headed to the kitchen, there was a knock at the door.

"Leslie, open the door," Mathias yelled.

"Mathias," she uttered, unlocking the door. "What are you doing here?"

"I was trying to come over so we could talk, but my key wouldn't work."

Leslie folded her arms. "That's because I changed the locks. You don't live here anymore, remember?"

Mathias tucked his key back into his pocket. "We should talk."

"Where are my children since you're here?"

"They're at my mother's house. She hadn't seen them in a while, so I dropped them off so she could spend some time with them. I figured it was the perfect time for us to chat without them being around."

"That was presumptuous of you, don't you think? Who said I was ready to have a conversation with you?"

"Leslie," he sighed. "How long are we going to do this before we finally talk things out?"

"I don't know...as long as it takes me to get past the fact a strange woman showed up at my door...our door, Mathias, with a child!" she yelled.

Mathias shamefully lowered his head. He knew this wasn't going to be a walk in the park, but he'd hoped that she would've at least been open to them talking at this point. He wasn't expecting her to be calm, but he wasn't expecting full outright resistance either.

"Can I come in so we can talk? I don't want to do this for all the neighbors to see."

Leslie scoffed at his request. She had no intention of letting him stay, but she would entertain whatever he had to say momentarily. Maybe this was her way of getting the answers she needed to decide what to do regarding their marriage.

She stepped back. "Come in."

Entering behind her, Mathias closed the door. Leslie stopped a few feet from where he stood and faced him. She didn't want him to get too comfortable or come too far inside, so she decided to remain standing. Picking up on her cold demeanor, Mathis took his cue from her.

"You wanted to talk, so talk," Leslie instructed.

"Leslie…I…I'm sorry," he began. "I never meant to hurt you in that way. Trust me when I say I know what I did was wrong and disrespectful, and I'm sorry for that. These past few days, I've really been doing some soul-searching, and I don't want to lose you."

Leslie grunted dismissively. "I don't trust anything you have to say, Mathias. Not one single thing because you've shown me you can't be trusted. You lied to me. To make matters worse, you embarrassed me. And then there's the fact that if she hadn't showed up at this door, I'd still be in the dark about who she is."

"Leslie, I don't want to lose my family."

"You should've thought about *our* family—" she air quoted harshly— "when you violated our marriage vows. But you didn't because our so-called family was the last thing that crossed your mind when you slept with her. Why should I believe it matters to you now?"

Mathias stared directly at her. "Because it does, and truthfully, it always has. I just…I got caught up in the attention. I strayed from what I knew was right, and I let my temptations get the best of me."

"How many? How many times did you let your temptations get the best of you? How many times did you sleep with her?"

"I'm not sure," he admitted.

"What?" Leslie asked. She barely got the words out of her mouth without gagging. A part of her needed to know, but there was the other part that was sickened to even hear what he was about to say. "You're not sure because it was that many times that you lost count, or you're not sure because you didn't even bother to?"

"It happened quite a few times, so I don't remember," he revealed.

"And I assume all of them *weren't* protected."

He shook his head. "Not all of them."

Leslie felt the knot in her stomach tightens. Knowing didn't feel any better than not knowing. It carried the same, if not more, pain. Breathing in and out, Leslie debated whether or not she was going to press forward or leave well enough alone. Her knowing he defiled their marriage should be enough. Still, she felt she needed to know more.

"So how can you honestly say that child isn't yours? How would you even know, Mathias?"

Silence echoed as Mathias thought about what she'd said.

"How many women were there?"

"Leslie," he said, almost pleading with her.

She shouted. "No! Don't Leslie me… answer my question. How many women were there? One…two…six? How many damn women?" she screamed.

Mathias hesitated.

"I'm waiting. The longer you take, the more I'm going to assume you're thinking of a damn lie. You came here wanting to talk to me, so tell me what I want to know," she demanded.

"Does it really matter?"

She huffed, concluding the number was probably about to knock the wind out of her. He was stalling. Classic Mathias. Whenever she'd catch him doing something, then ask about it, he'd stall. She eventually learned that he needed time to think of a lie.

"Yes, it matters. It matters because I want to know how many times you disrespected me, and with how many women."

"Four," he answered reluctantly.

Leslie gasped as she fought for air. She expected him to say one. She was even bracing herself for two, but four? Four were excessive. Outlandish. A far cry from him making a mistake. How could he betray her four times over? Did he really expect her to come to terms with that? And forgive him for all of them...really?

Leslie scowled at him. Her anger violently collided with heartache and her love for him. She felt stupid, vulnerable, and exposed. Was she the last to know? Who else knew? How many people knew her husband's dirty little secret while she was in the dark? Questions, reasonings, assumptions— one after the other, she mentally sorted through them. There were so many facets to betrayal. So many components that come into play. The angles. The plot. The deception. Layer after layer, she was forced to slice through in order to get to the root of it all.

"When did they start? When did you start cheating on me again?"

"Again?" he asked, astounded by her response.

"Yes…again! Let's not forget about the time I caught you before I had Micah," she pointed out.

Mathias scratched his head. "Baby, I don't have an exact timeline."

"Don't call me baby. And yes, you do. When did it start again?"

"About two years after we started the church," he solemnly admitted.

She did the math inside of her head. That was nine years ago. A year before, she had Lauren. Leslie thought back to what they had going on during that time. If she recalled, it was around the time she was thinking about going back to school, but he was adamant about starting the church. Then shortly after, she got pregnant, so once again, she postponed her dreams.

"I think it's time for you to leave, Mathias," she said, forcing the cry she felt surfacing back down. She didn't want to cry in front of him. "Leave, now!"

His face soured. "You asked me to be honest, then you punish me for it?"

"Punish you? Are you being serious right now? You just admitted you fu—" Leslie took a deep breath— "you literally admitted you slept with four women, and you expect me to be understanding and kind about that? Mathias, how would you feel if I told you that Myles, Micah, or any of our children weren't yours? Imagine how you would feel learning that I slept with another man, had his child, then pretended that child was yours? Now take that and multiply it times four, and that's how I feel right now!" she glared at him. "You don't get to make me feel bad about punishing you or whatever the hell you want to call it. Now get out of my house!"

A defeated look flooded his face.

"Leslie, I want to come back home. I want to make this right. Whatever it takes, I want my family back."

"Do you honestly expect me to forgive what you've done? One affair would've been hard enough, but four? Four, Mathias! Then let's not forget there's a child to factor in!"

"That child is not mine. I'm telling you the truth."

Leslie cut her eyes at him, dismissing the fact he yet again denied his part in the child's conception. "Do you even know what that is? You've lied to me for what...five, six...I don't know...eight years, maybe? Who knows at this point?"

"I'm willing to do whatever it takes to get my family back," he proclaimed. "Whatever it takes, Leslie. I'm not giving up on us."

"Maybe you should, all things considered. Apparently, you already have."

"I never loved any of them," he confessed.

"Is that supposed to make me feel better? The fact you didn't love them, but you repeatedly had sex with them. You felt something because you did it over-and-over again."

Sighing, he said, "What do you need me to do?"

Mathias remained silent. To him, it was, but clearly, it hadn't. Leslie looked at him, then looked away. She shook her head slightly to gather herself. She wasn't going to give him the satisfaction of her tears. He didn't deserve them.

Leslie pointed at her door. She glared at him. Her eyes were glazed over with a layer of moisture blended with fury. His begging carried no weight right now. All she cared to hear was the sound of her door closing behind him.

"I need you to leave. Right now, I need time to process all of this. I was already trying to come to terms with one, and now I have to contend with three more; I need time, Mathias."

"Leslie…"

"Goodbye, Mathias. Please don't come back without calling."

"That's it? You put me out without so much as telling me how to fix this?"

"There's nothing to fix."

"Can we go to marriage counseling?"

Leslie turned around and opened the door.

"All these solutions when all you had to do was keep your penis inside of your pants. No, Mathias. I don't want to go to counseling. I want you to leave and give me time to figure out what I want to do." She waved her hand, ushering him out the door. "Goodbye, and don't come back unless it's to drop off the kids."

CHAPTER FIFTEEN

Rolling over, Grace gazed at the clock. Wearily, she groaned at the fact she was up at five. So much had occurred since she arrived it'd become hard for her to rest without something disrupting her sleep.

What happened after she revealed the truth to Daniel added to her restlessness. She'd replayed their conversation over constantly, always arriving at the same conclusion; he would never forgive her now that he knew the truth. The pride he took in being a father to Sydney assured her of that. The guilt he felt about their past decision was all she'd been wrestling with.

She'd done that to him.

She robbed him of the opportunity to spend time with Alexis like she had. And that's the part she knew he'd never overlook. All this time, she'd been here—a few miles away—within arm's reach, and Grace didn't bother to say anything.

Then there was Alexis. She'd damaged their relationship severely, and she wasn't sure they'd ever come to an amicable resolution. She was preparing to tell her the truth, but she feared things would never be the same after this.

Turning over, she stared out of the window. The sky was still a canvas of black, but she could see traces of indigo peeking through as the sun began to push itself above the horizon. Something so peaceful, yet chaos trampled across her mind. She sighed.

Her eyes followed the fan blades as they rotated, blowing the cool air throughout the room. For some reason, the silent movement calmed her. She stared at them for a few minutes before light cut through the darkness in her room. Grace glanced over to her right, where her phone sat on the nightstand.

Reaching for it, she lifted it slightly to see it was an email from her assistant. She'd been on hiatus to deal with everything regarding her family and had told everyone not to disturb her unless it was absolutely important. If she was getting an email, it must've been important. Placing the phone down, Grace eased out of bed.

There was no way she was going back to sleep, so she might as well get up. She figured she'd enjoy watching the sunrise in the meantime. She grabbed her robe on the bench and slid her feet into her house shoes. Picking up a few items on her way, she went to the kitchen. She was in desperate need of something strong to drink, but coffee would have to suffice for now. The house was quiet and somewhat dark. The closer she got to the kitchen, the specks of light began casting a shadow along the walls. Dawn had arrived, and it wouldn't be long before the entire sky was lit up. A new day. Another chance for her to right a wrong.

Grace placed her phone and the papers down on the table next to where she left her computer, then moved toward where she knew her mother kept what she'd need to make some coffee. Her mother was an early riser, so she'd make enough for the

217

both of them. By the time Rose got it, it'd probably be cold, so she could make her own.

The aroma of dark-roasted beans wafted up her nose as she scooped spoonsful of it into the stainless-steel coffeemaker. Her dad loved vintage stuff he had in his childhood, so her mother always managed to find updated versions of them. Grace pressed the button to start the coffee. Making her way back to the table, she quietly pulled out a chair and sat down. Grace picked up the paper and unfolded it.

This one piece of paper had been the reason for all the disruption amongst her family lately. That and the lie centered around it. Grace stared at the letters that proved she was, in fact, Alexis's mother. She'd never seen this copy or the phony version her parents had drawn up to cover up the deceit they forced her to be a part of. Truth be told, she never bothered searching for it either. There was no point in it. The day she signed those adoption papers, she relinquished the right to know anything. Only it seemed she couldn't relinquish everything.

The coffee maker made a grunting noise, indicating it was finished making the caffeinated concoction she was ready to indulge in to begin her day. Grace poured her coffee and then went back to where she was seated, returning her attention back to the birth certificate. Her eyes roamed to the empty space next to hers where Daniel's name should've been but wasn't. He'd already signed his rights over before Alexis was born, so her parents felt his name didn't need to be included.

Her parents, she thought, huffing.

It's crazy how when she was younger, she believed they knew everything. Even what was best for her, but oh how wrong she was. At the time, they might've thought their decision was best for her, but Grace wholeheartedly felt they never considered the long-term effects it would have on her. Never once did they think about how this one instance would forever change how she connected to people if she'd ever be able to love again.

Because of their decision, Grace formed a complex about motherhood and relationships. She created walls because the burden of feeling that pain again wasn't something she cared to experience again.

Grace stared at her reflection in the mirror, rubbing her hand over her stomach. It had returned to its normal shape, but it was empty. Void of the life she hid inside of it for nine months. It matched how she felt inside. And the blankness people saw when they looked into her eyes. A year had gone by, but nothing about this place felt like home anymore. The warmth she once felt had long disappeared. The stable foundation she used to feel beneath her feet was now shaky. All she wanted to do was run as far away from here as she could.

She could stand to be around anyone anymore. Her parents. Her siblings. Daniel. No one. She couldn't think of a single soul that made her want to stay. Not even her. A light tap on the door interrupted her thoughts.

"Gigi," her mother called out.

220

Grace briefly closed her eyes for a moment. Her mother's voice used to be soothing. Now she dreaded hearing it, and every time she did, it felt like the knife was being dug in further. Sighing, she opened her eyes and said, "Yes."

"You done in there yet? It's almost time for you girls to get to school."

Grace swallowed and stared at herself one last time. She only had a few more months, and she'd be far away from here and anything that reminded her of this place. Opening the door, she saw her mother standing in the doorway. A faint smile formed across her lips before her eyes traveled to her stomach. Grace swallowed again, pushing the cry she'd been suppressing for months down. Inside was a little girl slated to arrive soon. Another member of their family. Another 'sister.' Another reminder of what happened.

"Gigi," her mother repeated, snapping her out of her emotional spiral.

Grace glanced at her mother, trying with all her might to keep it together. She'd had a few outbursts since it all happened, and it didn't go over well. Resulting in her stuffing her feelings as far down as possible so she could play the dutiful daughter.

"There's food if you're hungry," her mother told her.

Right as she was about to speak, Alexis wobbled over to her mother and started tugging at her robe. Her brown doe-eyes stared up at Grace before looking at her mother.

"Ma Ma," she cooed.

Grace's chest tightened every time she heard her say that. Unable to stand there any longer, she nodded at her mother, and eased out of the bathroom. Suddenly, the air in between them became hard to breathe in.

"Gigi…Gigi…you, okay?" her mother shook her and asked.

Grace blinked, not realizing anyone had woken up. She turned her head toward the kitchen where her mother had walked. She must've drifted off into deep thought.

"Yes," she finally said.

"You sure? I called your names a couple of times."

Grace nodded. "Just thinking about something Daniel said," she lied. She pushed the birth certificate to the side and pulled her computer closer.

"Must've been something intriguing. You were in pretty deep thought."

You have no idea, Grace thought, opening her email. She needed to see what her assistant had sent her. As much as she wanted to continue her hiatus, Grace was starting to feel going back to work was the only thing that would help take her mind off of everything. It also gave her an excuse to get the hell away from Deridder. Being her was dredging up stuff she wanted to keep buried for her sake and everyone involved.

Clicking open her email, she saw it was a job lead. As she read over the details, her mother joined her at the table. Out of the corner of her eye, she saw her pick up the birth certificate. Grace continued reading the screen, pretending not to notice. The two of them had never really talked about this or made amends for the decision made. Part of Grace had reconciled with the fact they never would a long time ago. But there was a small piece of her that wished they would. Maybe it was the little girl inside of her. Or perhaps, it was the longing for the love she yearned to have but didn't trust.

"How did he take the news?"

"As bad as you can imagine," Grace murmured.

"I figured as much when I saw you come in from your dinner with him."

Grace scoffed under her breath how her mother could say that when all of this was her fault— the decision they made—the lies, baffled her. This wasn't necessarily when she wanted to have this conversation, but since Rose was asleep, she figured it was best. Grace gazed at her mother.

"Was it easy for you? To decide to take my child away from me? Was that easy for you and

Daddy because it sure felt like it was," she blurted out.

Aurelie sipped her coffee. She knew this moment would come. She'd hoped her husband would be here for them to have it together, but he wasn't. And things didn't always happen how she wanted them to, so here they were. Placing her mug down, she placed her hand on top of Grace's and replied, "No, it wasn't. Not at all."

Grace slid her hand from beneath her mother's. She didn't believe her. In the depths of her soul, she felt to add insult to injury; they adopted Alexis. Only compiling that pain with more by getting pregnant with Mackenzie. It was one betrayal after the next.

"Gigi, that was the hardest decision I had to make as a parent. But I wouldn't change it. Look at what you've accomplished, all that you've become, what Daniel accomplished. Being a parent would have made it that much harder for you, the both of you," she added.

"But you didn't even give me a chance." Grace's voice cracked. "Who knows what would've happened," she protested.

"That may be true, but Gigi...do you think you could've still attended school on a full scholarship with a baby in tow? How would you have provided for her? Where would you have lived? Certainly not on campus, which means you would've had to get an apartment. Which also means you would've had to get a job. Do you have any idea how hard it would've been to work a full-time job—because that's what kind of job you needed—and be a full-time student?"

Grace looked away. Squeezing her eyes tightly to calm her emotions. Her mother's justification of her actions didn't negate the pain she caused her. In some instances, she understood, but in others, she didn't want to. They turned her into a liar. And they broke her heart.

"I get that, but still... taking my choice away from me made me feel like you didn't think I could do it. For years, I felt as though you thought you'd be a better mother than I would, and it hurt. It destroyed me to come into this house every day and watch you love on the child I brought into this world while thinking, was I not good enough?"

Aurelie grabbed Grace's hand, cuffing it tightly before placing a soft kiss on it. "No, Gigi. That wasn't the case at all. I never thought you weren't capable of loving Lexi, but you were a child yourself. Gigi, you were sixteen. What kind of mother would I have been to let you trot across the country at eighteen with a toddler?"

"I guess we'll never know, will we? You and Daddy got to enjoy all the good parts, all the first times and things I never got to cherish because I had to pretend they weren't mine. And now, I get the privilege of carrying the burden of the lie and deceit I was forced into. I have to be the one to unveil the truth and be the one everyone resents."

Silence floated between them for a few seconds as they gazed at each other. Her mother squeezed her hand tighter. Grace tried reasoning with herself—asking herself if the tables were turned and if it were Alexis pregnant at that age—would she have made the same decision? Would she have stolen Alexis's opportunity to decide for herself?

Perspective was one thing; reality was another.

"I wanted to tell Alexis," her mother admitted, "But your father told me that the choice to do so should be left up to you. I protested and pushed back, considering it was we who ultimately made the decision. I told him it would be better if it came from us, but he believed you should be left with that decision and whether or not it came out. I didn't agree with it, but I stood by him."

Grace sneered. "Sure he did." Grace loved her father, but his '*my way or the highway*' motto when they were growing up was hard to deal with. Mainly because he always felt he knew better.

"I'm sorry, Gigi. I'm sorry that you felt I didn't think you were good enough. I'm sorry that you believed I doubted your ability to be a fantastic mother because that wasn't the case at all. Mostly,

228

I'm sorry for robbing you of an opportunity to be a mother."

Grace got choked up. For years, she wondered what she would feel like hearing those words. She'd given up on hearing them, figuring they never thought what they did was wrong; therefore, waiting around for them to admit it was pointless. Now here, her mother was pushing her pride to the side and doing what she never thought she'd do.

"You know what hurts the most is that Daniel didn't even give me a chance to explain things to him. He didn't even want to hear my side of things. And the way he looked at me…it was like I was Judas himself. He's never going to forgive me."

Aurelie caressed Grace's hand. "Gigi, I know what we did caused you to keep your distance. I'll admit, it tore me up inside that you didn't come home for six years after you left. But I understood. Something told me the day we dropped you off at the airport; we wouldn't see you for a

229

long time. The resentment you'd been harboring. The way you moved around the house, like you despised being here, I felt it in my spirit. I knew I would have to make peace with that because you wouldn't until you were ready to come home."

Grace wiped the tears off her cheek. This was not how she saw her morning going. She sat in silence, allowing her mother's words to resonate. She was conflicted. Her mother's words felt sincere, heartfelt even. But it was as if the betrayal wouldn't loosen its grip on her. In a way, she understood Daniel's reaction. His anger came from a dark place. One she was very acquainted with. Her mother gently swiped her along her cheek, and a wave of peace passed over her.

"Gigi, I want you to know that me and your father were proud of you. We were, no… we are proud of how despite everything that occurred, you went out into the world and became this phenomenal photographer—traveling and seeing places we've only dreamt of. Watching you do all that allowed us to have some peace about what we chose to do."

Grace nodded, unable to speak.

Her mother rose and stood next to Grace. Wrapping her arms around her, Aurelie pressed Grace's head into her chest. The steady sound of her mother's heartbeat echoed in her ear. Grace exhaled slowly in her mother's embrace while she caressed her cheeks. There was something soothing about her touch, a comforting feeling she hadn't felt in a long time.

"Secrets have consequences, Gigi. Inevitable consequences that have a way of destroying things. Your father and I realized that when you left, and again whenever you'd come home, and you and Leslie would be at each other's throats. We did that, and I will take full responsibility for that. But now you get the opportunity to be better than we were. You get the chance to mend your relationship with your sisters," she kissed Grace's forehead tenderly. "And you get a chance to have that relationship with Lexi that you want if you want it."

"Ma, Lexi's never going to see me as a mother," Grace expressed. "And Daniel…well, that's a whole different story altogether."

"Gigi, you always did think you knew everything," Aurelie said and smiled. "How about this time, you leave a little room for possibilities. Life has a way of surprising you. Give it a chance to. You never know; people just might be open to forgiveness."

Grace nodded.

"Whatever you need from me, I'm here. All I want is for you to forgive yourself, and when you've done that, forgive me and your father."

Grace closed her eyes. Forgiveness was harder to swallow than betrayal, but she knew she had to do it. If she wanted forgiveness, she was going to have to extend it. Her parents had apologized, and even though her heart was a long way from being mended, it was a start.

And for now, that would do.

CHAPTER SIXTEEN

Jasper had been parked in the same spot for the past hour. He'd gotten out early, carefully trailing Mackenzie's mother into town; he didn't know how much longer his patience would hold up. He'd been watching her house from a distance since his first visit, patiently waiting for Mackenzie to surface, but he'd had no luck. A couple of times, he contemplated knocking on their door again, hoping to catch them off guard, but he decided on this approach instead. Plus, there hadn't been so much as an inkling of her presence near the residence, so he figured she was laying low somewhere else around town.

One of her sisters, he couldn't recall her name, left days ago. He concluded she might've returned to wherever she lived since when the other one came back, she was in the car alone. He was amazed at how oblivious people were to their surroundings. None of them had even noticed his car near their house. Nor had her mother paid attention to the fact he'd been hopping in and out of the car to follow her with each stop she'd made. Jasper was certain Mackenzie was still here. And he was even more certain they were keeping her hidden.

Their loyalty and devotion were admirable. Foolish but admirable. Dangerous even, but he respected their unbreakable family ties. However, his willpower superseded their loyalty. All he had to do was bide his time. She'd surface sooner or later, and when she did, he would get his money. Mackenzie was trotting around with nearly a million dollars of his hard-earned money and wanted it back.

And since she was making it incredibly difficult, he would have to incentivize her because running across the country, chasing her for it, was not working. He needed to bait her, and what better person to draw her out than her mother? Jasper unlocked his phone to check the cameras at his house. He'd been doing this periodically since he left since he didn't fully trust people. Plus, he also wasn't sure who was watching his comings and goings, so to be sure nothing in his house was removed, he checked the cameras.

He did the same at the shop.

Finding out that Mackenzie was conspiring with Nina, he had cameras installed after hours. No one knew about them, and he wanted it kept that way. Oftentimes people showed their true colors when they didn't think anyone was watching. Eventually, Mackenzie would call her, and the minute she did; he wanted to know. Nina was his plan b if she didn't surface soon.

Jasper held his camera up to zoom in closer. He needed to capture the perfect picture to send to Mackenzie. Pressing the button, he snapped a few pictures of her mother. She'd turned around a couple of times, giving him a couple of frontal views, making identifying her a lot easier. As he took the pictures, he noticed an officer walking in his direction. Lowering his phone, he adjusted in his seat just in case he was the target of the officer's curiosity. His eyes followed the man, and as he suspected, he stopped at Jasper's car.

Tapping on the window with his knuckle, he took a step back as he waited for Jasper to lower his window. To help speed this up, Jasper complied. He didn't know what the officer could've wanted, but hopefully, he'd be more of a help instead of a pain in the ass. Smiling, Jasper greeted him, "Hello, Officer. Is everything ok?"

"Hello, and yes. I've been observing from over there—" he pointed across the street to his car that was behind a couple of cars— "I just noticed you've been parked here for a while. Are you waiting on someone?"

Jasper forced a feeble smile as he pondered over the response he wanted to give. It'd be a lie, of course, still, it needed to be believable and convincing enough that the officer would be on his way. He still had Mackenzie's mother in his peripheral vision, making sure she didn't stray too far or someone else met up with her.

"Ahem," the officer cleared his throat.

"Sorry, officer, I saw my mother-in-law out and about, and I was about to catch up with her," he lied.

"Who's your mother-in-law?" he inquired.

"Mrs. Bayou," Jasper answered, unsure of her first name. Something else he realized was odd, considering how long he and Mackenzie had been together. But she rarely ever said her first name, referring to her as Ma, so he never thought to ask. "She's just up the way, and I'm waiting here. I was hoping my wife would be with her." Jasper flashed him another smile, a friendlier one so he'd appear truthful.

The officer took another step back and peeked into his car. He had a peculiar look on his face, one that made Jasper leery. "And which sister are you married to again?" he asked, vetting Jasper's story. "Because, to my recollection, only one of them is married."

Jasper arched a brow, curious to how familiar he was with their family. Evidently, everyone in this godforsaken town knew their family. Now he understood why Mackenzie ran for the nearest highly populated city she could get to—all of them, honestly. It was too small. And boring, definitely boring. He'd been here close to two weeks, and aside from eating, there wasn't much for people to do here. Nothing other than tending to other people's business.

"I'm Mackenzie's husband," he answered.

"Mickey!" his voice amplified. "Mickey, as in Mackenzie Bayou, is married? You're telling me you're married to little Mackenzie Bayou?"

The grin on his face left Jasper bewildered. He wasn't sure if he was surprised or enthralled to know she was spoken for. Jasper watched him go through his range of emotions, wondering if he might've had a thing for her himself.

"Yes, Mackenzie Bayou. We've been married for about four years now."

"Oh wait," he said as if a thought crossed his mind. Then he pointed at Jasper, "You're the one who reported her missing, right? I forgot... I did something around the station regarding her alleged disappearance."

Jasper nodded.

"Did you find her? I was wondering since she was clearly not missing. I figured it was a mistake when the sheriff mentioned it. Especially the part about her being married." The officer shook his head. "Well, I'll be. I had no idea Mickey was married. I just saw her, and she didn't say a thing," he stated.

Jasper's ears perked up. "Oh yeah," he said, trying to decide which angle he was going to play. "That sounds like Mickey. Always keeping secrets. You must've seen her around here somewhere. "She's been everywhere since being back," he alluded.

"Yep, saw her in town a couple of times. The first time it was with her sister. Then again, a couple of days ago, when she was with Carter. They grabbed some food at the White Elephant, and then I saw her the next day walking out of the Blue Moon."

Who the hell is Carter Reed? Jasper wondered.

"A couple of days ago, huh?" Jasper confirmed, thinking that wasn't too long after he first showed up at her parents' house. "We had a little fight, and it seems she's still upset with me. You know how that goes. They get mad and give you the silent treatment. I'm trying to get back in her good graces by chauffeuring my mother-in-law around."

"Yeah, I do. My lady is the same way...overdramatic," he laughed.

"That's an understatement," Jasper agreed.

"That Mickey has always been a wild card," he said, smiling.

Jasper gritted his teeth. For the sake of needing information, he would overlook the officer's obvious infatuation with his wife. He didn't want to bother asking if they dated. In a town of this size, it wouldn't surprise him. He went back to what he said about her staying at her sister's house. He hadn't thought about how that was another option since she always said they were scattered across the country. He automatically assumed all of them had moved elsewhere.

Obviously, one of them didn't.

"Well, I'll let you get back to your outing. If I see Mickey, I'll tell her you're looking for her," the officer told him.

"Thanks, I appreciate it."

"No problem. Enjoy your day," the officer waved and walked the other way.

Jasper returned the wave and raised his window. Once the officer was a distance away, he searched for her mother again, upset that she was gone. The officer's account of the last time he saw her led Jasper to believe she might've hidden somewhere long enough until she felt it was safe enough. More than ever, he was positive she was back at that house. His patience was growing thinner by the minute.

"Let's see where you're hiding, Mackenzie," he murmured.

Glancing down at his phone, Jasper opened his browser and typed *Blue Moon* in the search bar. Instantly, results of all kinds popped up, but the one that stood out the most was the first option— The Blue Moon Motel. Clenching his jaw, Jasper took several deep breaths. The caged rage brewing was slowly teetering near the edge.

"Alright, Mickey. You're at motels with men, huh," he mumbled to himself. "Okay, Mickey, I see what you're up to. Let's play."

Jasper cleared his browser, opening his photo album and locating the photos he'd taken of her mother. Clicking the share option, he selected the email option to send her a message since he had no phone number for her. Adding all the attachments, he typed, *Mackenzie, you can do this the easy way or hard way. Either way, I'm going to get you and my money back.*

Jasper hit send and sat his phone down. He started the car and pulled off. First, he was headed to the Blue Moon to see if she was still there. And then, he went back to her parents' house to pay

242

them another visit because he was certain she was still here.

CHAPTER SEVENTEEN

"Reservation for Bayou," Rose told the hostess.

"How many," the hostess asked.

"Should be for three," she confirmed.

"Okay, one moment."

The hostess scrolled the list on her tablet to locate Rose's reservation. After the lineup debacle, Rose had cleared her house of any reminders of Lucien, ordered her some more furniture, decided on some new paint colors, and moved on. In doing so, she managed to catch up with a few of her friends. Balancing friendships, a significant other, and a busy career had gotten to be a lot, and unfortunately, her friendships took the brunt of that.

Now that she was single again, not to mention unemployed—she had plenty of free time until she decided what she wanted to do. At this point, she wasn't sure if she wanted to go through all the rigamarole of cleaning up her resume and then going through the motions of interviewing. The entire spectacle of proving she's qualified while navigating sexism, ageism, and whatever other form of discrimination seemed exhausting.

"Oh! I have you right here," she said, locating Rose's name.

"Have the other people arrived yet?"

"Yes, they have. Right this way?" she instructed. "Meredith, I'll be right back. I'm going to seat her."

The other young lady nodded as I walked around the podium to follow her. We walked through the dining room tables as she led her to the patio. She always loved Toulouse Café & Bar, and today was the perfect day to come. It was cool in Houston today. The sun was out, but it wasn't hot like it normally was this time of year.

"Your dress is gorgeous," someone told her as she passed.

Rose mouthed, "Thank you," as she continued following the hostess.

While she was remodeling her house, she decided to revamp her wardrobe as well. The flowy, floral number she had on was one of her new pieces. She felt whimsical in it as it lightly blew in the wind, drawing attention to her exquisitely toned legs. Despite her lack of social interaction, Rose always made time for the gym. It was another thing she and Lucien had in common.

"Rosie!" Evelyn shouted, standing up to hug her.

"Eve!" she shouted, then whispered, "Thank you," to the waitress.

She smiled and nodded, then disappeared back inside.

Rose turned her attention back to her friend and old colleague, hugging her tight. She hadn't spoken to anyone since she left Martin Advertising, having to go straight to Deridder. There was so much they had to catch up on. Releasing her, Rose embraced Sophia next. She'd known both of them for close to twenty-five years, having met Sophia upon her arrival in Houston. She met Sophia during a summer internship at her first ad agency.

They instantly hit off, becoming fast friends. A few years later, she met Evelyn when she joined the team at Martin Advertising. The three of them became the three amigas in no time flat—traveling, shopping, and dancing their nights away while having their way with the city of Houston.

"You look amazing!" Sophia complimented her. "Lucien must really be wooing you because you're glowing."

Rose blushed to keep from frowning. She was happy she didn't look like what she'd been through these past two months. "Girl, thank you, you look spectacular yourself. You too, Eve," she replied, tapping her on the arm. Rose skirted past the Lucien reference. She was going to need a few mimosas before she tackled that topic.

Evelyn sipped her mimosa. "Two weeks in Turks & Caicos will do that to you."

"So will a husband who flies you wherever you want to go, whenever you want to go," Sophia teased.

"Cut it out, Sophie. We all know Kent will whisk you away at the drop of a hat," Evelyn waved her off.

They all laughed.

"Woo, I'm jealous. I could use a vacation right about now," Rose said.

"Take one. I mean, it's not like you can't afford it. For goodness sake, your fiancé is a pilot and can fly you to any destination in the world," Sophia added.

Rose snickered, picking up the carafe and champagne flute to pour some of the mimosa. They were already starting with the Lucien references. Filling it almost to the brim, Rose sat the carafe down and sipped her drink.

"What's been up with you two?" she asked, redirecting the conversation from her. "We haven't talked in a month of Sundays."

"That's because you've been held up in that house with that fine man. Y'all acting like newlyweds, and you haven't even jumped the broom yet, or have you?" Evelyn teased, eyeing her.

"You know you're good for doing things under the radar, then popping up like no time has passed."

Rose swatted her friend. "You know what, how many of these has she had already?" she glanced at Sophia, "Because she's acting up."

Sophia laughed. "This is our second carafe. We're way ahead of you. You need to catch up!"

"Is there a party or something we're headed to that I don't know about? Why are we on the second carafe?" Rose laughed.

"We aren't on anything. As Sophie said, you need to catch up, missy. Also, figure out what you want to eat; the waitress should be back soon."

Rose scoured the menu, mentally sorting through what she wanted to eat. Everything looked so good in the description. She'd noticed the menu had been updated since a few of the items listed she didn't recognize. She decided in the nick of time. As soon as she looked up, the waitress was headed toward their table. The three of them rattled off their selections, along with another mimosa carafe, then returned to their conversation.

"Tell me Evie, how's things at Martin Advertising since I've been gone?"

"Nope don't even try it," Evelyn interrupted. "We are not going to talk about that crazy place. Fill us in on that sexy fiancé of yours."

"About that—" she held out her ringless finger— "we're not getting married. Lucien and I are no longer engaged. And before either of you ask why, I found out he wasn't who he said he was. While together, he pretended to be a man named Lucien Jarreau, but his real name was Xavier Conway. He stole from me, cleared my house of quite a few things—my bank account too, and he's now being held in the Houston County Jail."

Silence reverberated amongst them. No one said anything, allowing her recount of recent events to take up the space needed for her to heal and recover from them. Rose held her head high like always.

"Oh my God, Rosie," Sophia stood, rushing her with a hug. "I'm so sorry; we didn't know. Why didn't you say anything?" she released her.

"I was going to but I had so much else going on with my father, then losing my job. Lucien, or, shall I say, Xavier, wasn't a priority. I had to compartmentalize my tragedies," she chuckled. "But I'm good now, and I don't want to rehash it anymore. He's no longer in my life and now that I have a fresh start, I will do just that."

Sophia held up her glass. "A toast…to Rose and her fresh start. May this new chapter bring you better opportunities and new love?"

Rose and Evelyn picked up their glasses. "To new beginnings," they said in unison.

They sipped their drinks, and Rose smiled inwardly. Thank God she had supportive friends because , her sisters' lives were in shambles right now and they couldn't be here for her like they normally would.

"Alright, what's next?" Sophia asked. "What is the next chapter going to be?"

"It's funny you said that. I was thinking…"

"Miss Bayou?" a masculine voice interrupted.

Rose peered over her shoulder and found Detective Graves standing there. She grinned, completely surprised to see him. Rose took in how incredible he looked in regular, casual clothes. Every time she'd seen him, he'd been in suits.

"Detective Graves? What are you doing here?.".""

"Who is that?" she heard Evelyn ask.

Rose smiled and kept her focus on Liam.

"Call me Liam. That's what I go by when I'm off the clock. I wasn't sure it was you when you first walked in, but we were on our way out, and I wanted to say hello."

"We?" Rose said before she could catch herself. She didn't mean to say it like that.

"Yes, a couple of friends of mine."

"Cops have friends. I thought everyone hated you guys," she teased.

He laughed. He was happy to see she hadn't let what happened to rob her of her sense of humor. Stroking his goatee, he replied, "We have a few. You know, we aren't cops twenty-four-seven."

"True enough. What are you up to on this fine Saturday?" she asked, trying to distract her mind from how delectable his lips looked. She hadn't paid much attention to them either time she'd seen him at the station, but for some reason, she couldn't stop staring at them now.

"Not much. Simply trying to enjoy this beautiful day. It's rare I get weekends off, so I'm making good use of my down time."

Rose nodded, thinking she was doing the same.

"I see you're out doing the same," he motioned to her friends.

"Oh…yes!" she said, remembering she had onlookers. "These are my best friends—Evelyn and Sophia; this is Detective Graves."

"Liam," he corrected.

"Right, sorry. This is Liam. He's the detective who helped me with my case."

Mischievous looks formed on their faces as they flashed girlish smiles at him. Rose did her best not to feed into it.

"Hello, Liam. I'm Evelyn," she said, holding her hand out.

"And I'm Sophia. So happy you were able to help our friend."

"Me too. Rose seems like a wonderful woman. I'm happy I was the one who could help resolve her problem."

Rose cleared her throat. Recognizing how the huskiness in his voice sounded different, she wondered if he was flirting.

The four exchanged a few more words, and then he turned to her. "Well, Rose, I'm going to let you get back to your friends. I'm sure mine are wondering where I disappeared to."

"Yes, it was nice seeing you again."

"You as well. I prefer this to meeting in the station."

There it is again, she thought.

An awkward silence floated between them for a few seconds before he asked, "Would you mind giving me your number? I wouldn't want to search through your case file to get it again, as it would be unethical. But I would love to see you on the personal side of things."

Rose hesitated. Unsure if she wanted to give him her number. He had a front-row seat to her tragic love story. She wasn't sure if was how she wanted to start a new relationship, nor was she entirely sure if she was ready for a new one.

"Ahem," Sophia cleared her throat. "He asked for your number, Rose."

Rose snapped out of her thoughts. "Yes, sorry."

Liam detected her reluctancy. After all, she'd just endured a horrible breakup and probably needed time to move past that situation. Deciding he'd put the ball in her court instead, he reached for his wallet and pulled out one of his business cards. "Does anyone have a pen?" he asked.

Evelyn quickly grabbed her purse hanging on the chair and ruffled through it until she found one. She handed it to him, and he smiled.

"Thank you," he told her. Liam jotted down his number and then handed the pen back to Evelyn.

She accepted and he turned his attention back to Rose. "Here—" he handed her the card— "I put my personal number on the back. How about you call me whenever you're ready. No pressure, but if you ever want to grab a coffee or dinner, give me a call."

"Will do," she answered.

"You ladies, enjoy the rest of your evening."

Rose watched him walk off, and once he disappeared, she sat back down. She took another sip of her mimosa, not missing the fact her friends were staring.

"You're not going to sit here and act like that fine specimen of a man didn't just ask you out on a date. What's up with you?" Evelyn asked, playfully tapping her arm.

"Did both of you forget what I just went through?" she asked.

"Sounds like the perfect pivot to me," Evelyn joked.

Sophia said, "Right…out with the old, in with the new!"

Rose laughed. "You two are nuts."

"We might be, but that hunk of a man is worth being a looney for," Sophia fanned herself. "Dear Lord, why does he hide all that deliciousness behind a uniform?"

Evelyn giggled as she took another sip.

"He's a detective crazy; he doesn't wear a uniform," Rose said.

Sophia frowned. "Bummer. I thought you could at least get some role-playing out of it. I mean, he does have handcuffs, at least, right?"

Rose shook her head. "Ma'am, who says I'm looking for a Christian Grey type?"

"I don't care what you say; Christian Grey was hot!" Evelyn added. "He could tie me up any day!"

They laughed as Rose stared down at the card still in her hand. She was reluctant about jumping into something new, but what the hell…who says she can't have a little fun on her road to happiness again.

CHAPTER EIGHTEEN

Mackenzie sat in the clinic's waiting room, scrolling through one of the many pregnancy magazines they had for people to read. Being back in Atlanta made her feel uneasy. Since she'd slid back into town, she'd been looking over her shoulders. Even though she was at least an hour from where she and Jasper lived, she still felt on edge. She was trying to be as invisible as possible, which is why she had Alexis reserve the rental car and the Airbnb in her name.

She'd given her enough cash to float her expenses for a month until Mackenzie was able to align some things. As a condition to help her get back in town, Alexis insisted she see an obstetrician. Mackenzie was apprehensive about it since she was trying to keep her pregnancy off the radar, but Alexis wasn't bending on her terms. Aware of how persistent her sister could be, Mackenzie caved, allowing her to arrange something with an old nursing school friend of hers who happened to live in Atlanta to help keep everything under wraps.

She'd done some research regarding divorce in Georgia, and everything that came back stated she would have to disclose she was pregnant; otherwise, there'd be some serious consequences. The last thing she needed was to be locked up for perjury because Jasper wasn't above doing that and then taking their child from her. Nervous, she tapped her foot against the floor.

More and more, she was beginning to realize why her parents would always instill in them, *"be careful who you have children with."* She regretted she didn't take that as seriously as she should have. Now she was here, trying to get an examination so she could at least ensure the child growing inside her was okay, even if she wasn't.

"First time, Mother?" the lady next to her whispered.

Mackenzie glanced at her and grinned. "Yeah, how'd you know?"

The lady pointed at her leg, lightly bouncing up and down. Mackenzie looked down at her leg, then stopped mid-tap before inhaling deeply. "Yeah," she admitted. "Guess I'm a little nervous."

Smiling, the woman next to her said, "We've all been there. Trust me when I say it gets a little easier, but not by much."

Mackenzie peered at her round belly. The way it was protruding, she looked to be in her second or third trimester. Oftentimes she wondered how big her stomach was going to get; where she would carry most of her weight; how much of her body would change, housing this life inside of her. Conflicting emotions passed through her. Mackenzie had never given a lot of thought to motherhood, but the few thoughts she had, she always imagined they would be happy. Never in a million years was this how she pictured her pregnancy. Running from the man she loved with money she stole from him. Not exactly a situation a child should be born into.

"I take it this isn't your first pregnancy," Mackenzie presumed.

"Nope, third," she said, beaming. Her hand moved back and forth over her stomach. "And it's another girl."

"That's wonderful," Mackenzie replied, ignoring the tinge of envy that coursed through her. Excitement was seeping through the woman's pores, and she hopelessly wanted a piece of it. If only for just a moment. "You seem excited."

The woman took the deepest breath. "Yes and no. I'm excited but ready for this part to be over. I'm exhausted, and I want my body back. I'm tired of sharing it."

She laughed, causing Mackenzie to smile.

"Are you hoping for a girl or boy?" the woman asked her.

"Honestly, I'm not sure what I want."

"Well, that's okay too. I was the same way this time around. I wanted a boy, but after the second girl, I was like, okay…whatever. Then we found out I was pregnant again. Of course, my husband tried to get me hyped up about having a boy, but I was like, I don't care—I just want these forty weeks or so to fly by." She chuckled as if a passing thought raced across her mind. "By the third one, the sex doesn't even matter anymore. You hope it's healthy and doesn't do anything crazy to your body."

Mackenzie flashed her another warm smile. Oddly enough, talking to the woman made her a little less nervous. She felt calm all of a sudden as if she needed to be around a kindred spirit or something. Mackenzie's eyes traveled to her hand, cuffing her belly. Her ring finger was missing her wedding ring, but she could still see traces of the line, indicating it used to be there. Mackenzie guessed it was probably because her fingers got swollen. She remembered reading something like that in another magazine she'd gotten a hold of.

"I think that's all I am wishing for… a healthy baby, that is."

"How far along are you? If you don't mind me asking."

Mackenzie shrugged, embarrassed by the fact she didn't know. "I'm not sure. That's why I'm here. I took a test a few weeks ago."

"Oh, you're probably in the early stages. You're not showing, so more than likely, you're still in your first trimester. Most of us don't find out until we're around or close to two months."

Mackenzie smiled inwardly. She appreciated the woman not judging her for her lack of knowledge. Admitting she didn't know she was pregnant might've garnered a different response, but she was gentle with her. Especially being a first-time mom and all.

"Good to know," she said softly.

The door to the back opened. "Ava Franklin," the nurse called out.

"That's me," the woman next to her said, raising her finger. Mackenzie watched as she gradually eased out of the chair. "Getting up isn't easy when you get to this point. Enjoy it while it lasts," she smiled at Mackenzie then snickered. "It was nice meeting you."

"Nice meeting you too. Congratulations on your baby as well. I hope you have a healthy delivery," Mackenzie told her.

"Same to you," she said, disappearing into the back.

Once the door closed, Mackenzie was left in the empty waiting room with nothing but her thoughts to tend to. The lobby music playing barely drowned out the phones ringing behind the window that separated them from her. Floating between her thoughts and the music, Mackenzie's phone rattled her. She hated that she was so jumpy, but Jasper showing up at her mother's had her on edge.

She fetched her phone from her purse. Hesitantly tapping on the screen, she saw the email notification. It was a message from Jasper. He didn't have any way of contacting her via phone, so this was his next best thing. She stared at the phone, debating if she was going to open it or not. Knowing him, it was another sadistic threat or comment. He was a full-blown narcissist, and she was doing her best not to let him affect her.

Figuring it was best to know the devil's every move, Mackenzie opened the email and saw there was an attachment and a message.

Scrolling down, she gasped at the image in front of her. Her eyes bulged as her heartbeat rapidly against her chest. She couldn't believe she was staring at a picture of her mother—out shopping, unbeknownst that she was being followed. Mackenzie moved the screen further down to read the text he added.

You can do this the easy way or the hard way. Either way, I'm going to get you and my money back.

Frozen, Mackenzie sat staring at her mother. He was still in Deridder. Still searching for her. Still under the guise that her family was hiding her when she wasn't there. Now he was threatening to harm her mother. And she knew it was more than a threat. She knew he'd make good on it. Mackenzie closed out the email to call her mother when she heard her name.

Mackenzie tapped her foot rapidly as the phone rang in her ear. First, Nina, now he was threatening her family. She hoped to God Jasper hadn't done anything crazy to her mother.

"Hello," her mother answered.

"Ma! Where are you?" she asked nervously.

"Mickey, what's wrong with you? Are you okay?"

"Not really. Where are you?" she repeated.

"I'm at home; why?"

Mackenzie exhaled the heavy breath she'd harbored. "Jasper, he sent me a picture of you. He was obviously following you."

Aurelie shouted, "What! Mickey, what the hell is going on with you and that man? And I want the truth, not the watered-down version you gave your sisters."

"It's a long story," she murmured.

"Well, start at the beginning, and don't leave anything out."

"Yes, ma'am," Mackenzie acknowledged. "Jasper and I…." Mackenzie began telling her mother about her secret marriage. Thank God no one was in the waiting room because of the shame she felt already. She didn't need to add the awkward glances of complete strangers. For the next several minutes, Mackenzie told her mother most of everything—leaving out the part about her being pregnant by the maniac—and her recent act of embezzlement. They didn't need to know everything.

"Mackenzie Bayou," someone called.

Looking up, she peered across the room to where the nurse was standing. She needed to call her mother and warn her to stay in the house. Jasper was on a rampage, and she knew he would scorch the earth with fire to get what she took from him back. His money. And his pride. The former more than later, but nevertheless, he felt the sting of both.

"Ma, I need to go. I'll call you later."

"No…wait! Mickey, where are you?"

"I'm back in Atlanta. I'll call you later when I get settled."

Mackenzie hung up and looked up.

"Mackenzie Bayou," the nurse repeated.

"Yes," she waved. "I'll be right back."

Jasper's knee-jerk reactions were the very reason she couldn't tell him she was pregnant. She couldn't risk him doing something drastic to her child. She had to fix this. Otherwise, she'd be running for the rest of her life, and that was no way to raise a child. She had a few more things to line up and thought she had a little more time, but it was clear she didn't.

Opening her email, she started typing. After finishing it, she glanced at her words one last time. *It's up to you, but I'm not there. Catch me if you can,* then she pressed send.

CHAPTER NINETEEN

Alexis turned the knob, reducing the intensity of the flame. Her house smelled like a fusion of spices and vegetables, creating the most mouthwatering aromas she'd ever smelled. She was cooking her father's favorite gumbo—a long-time family recipe—passed down for generations. It was one of the first things all of them learned how to cook; however, Alexis managed to perfect it better than her sisters.

"Mmm," she moaned, tasting the roux she'd spent countless hours refining.

It was finally the right consistency and color. She'd started with the holy trinity, and from there, she created layers of savory flavors. The seafood was fresh from the market she occasionally went to on weekends; she didn't have to work. Being the consummate chef he was, her father taught them all great dishes started with the best ingredients.

She placed the spoon down. "That's perfect…perfect."

Alexis smiled as the thought of her father standing next to her, saying those exact words flashed across her mind. Out of all of them, she was the one who enjoyed cooking with him. It was their way of bonding. He'd share stories of how and when he learned to cook a particular dish and she'd soak it all up, memorizing every single detail down to the number of times he shook a spice or scoops he'd make of whatever he was adding.

She peeked across the room at the box she'd been avoiding for the past week or so. Question after question circulated throughout her mind, yet she always came back to the same spot—she needed answers. If nothing else, she yearned to know if she was the only one or if she had siblings. Leaning on her quaint little island, she rested her head in her hand.

A knock on the door grabbed her attention. After looking through the peephole, she smiled while pulling it open. "You're early," she said, stepping back to let Keith in.

Grinning from ear-to-ear as he inhaled the aromatic scent filling her apartment, he walked in, and she closed the door behind him. "Oh, my goodness, it smells good. What are you cooking?"

"My daddy's gumbo," Alexis said, walking back to the kitchen. "I can take that if you like?"

She held her hand out for the bottle of wine Keith had brought. Surprised that he chose wine instead of their usual tequila or bourbon. *At least he brought red*, she thought, tucking it to the side. "Can I get you a glass?' she asked.

Keith shook his head as he pulled one of the stools out to sit down. "Water is fine right now. I can wait for dinner to drink the wine."

"Ice or no ice?"

"Just water is fine," he replied.

Alexis slid the glass in front of him and then turned to stir the gumbo. "It should just be a few more minutes, and we can eat. The rice is cooking now."

"I'm still shocked you invited me over. To be honest, I'm even more shocked that you know how to cook," he teased. "Who would've thought...Alexis Bayou...super nurse and a culinary connoisseur."

Alexis laughed. "Connoisseur is a stretch. But I can do a little something."

"I'm inclined to believe you. If it tastes as good as it smells, I'm in for a treat."

"I promise it does. Also, I invited you over to thank you for being here for me. You've been a great friend since I've been back; I appreciate it."

"I told you; I can be more than a booty call if you let me." Keith winked, taking a sip of water.

"You did."

"Speaking of which, how is that going, by the way? I know it's been a few days since I've asked. Did you ever get a hold of someone at the state office?"

Alexis placed the spoon down. "I did, and it's the same answer. They have no record of me being born in Deridder or in the state of Louisiana."

"Wow, that's really crazy. Have you spoken with anyone since you left??" he questioned.

"Actually, I've spoken to my sister Leslie since I told you what happened. She told me who my father was, so I have a name... Daniel Alexander," Alexis revealed. "I also spoke to my mother, but aside from her telling me why she and my father did what they did; she didn't budge on anything else."

Keith sensed a little sadness in her voice regarding her mother, but he was happy she at least got a name. It beats not knowing anything. He grinned at her. "That's great, Lexi!" he said excitedly. "Okay, what's next? Have you looked into who he is or where he might be?"

"No, I haven't, but I was seriously considering taking that," she pointed to the box still on her coffee table. "I think it will give me some idea of where he might be since I have a name. If not him, possibly a close relative who might know.

Keith turned around and saw the box she was pointing to. He frowned. The lengths she was being pushed to in order to find answers they could easily give her bothered him. He didn't know why, but something in him felt the need to protect her. Rescue her. Perhaps be a solution in her world of unanswered questions.

"Why haven't you opened it yet?" he asked, gazing back at her.

Alexis shrugged. "I don't know. Weird, isn't it?"

"Not necessarily. Sometimes the very thing we want to know scares us. The unknown can be frightening. You're opening Pandora's box, unsure of what lies inside, and once it's open, there's no going back. Are you sure you want to know?"

Alexis nodded. "Yes. It's like now that I know, I can't go back to pretending I don't. It'll eat away at me."

"Well then, take the test. You can do it now; I'll be right here with you. But the voices in your head aren't going to quiet the longer it sits there."

She sighed. He was right, and she knew it. She'd already spent the money, so she might as well take it and see what it told her. For all she knew, she could find some relatives that she could trace back to her biological father.

"Okay, I'll do it," she said, rounding the island to grab the box. "Besides, what's the worst I could find out?"

Keith didn't know how to answer that since it was a loaded question. There was a lot she could uncover—good or bad— which is why he said that tidbit about Pandora's box. But it wasn't for him to decide. Besides, he couldn't say how he'd handle this if he was in her shoes. The allure of the unknown was a hard thing to resist.

Alexis opened the box, pulling out its contents. Placing each item on the countertop, she unfolded the instructions and read over them. After a quick skim, she said, "Okay, so I need to swab my cheeks, put it back in here, then fill out some details. Once I do that, I'll mail it in and just wait."

"Do you want me to swab you?" he asked.

She blushed. "I wouldn't want you to do any strenuous activities while off the clock, Dr. Harper."

"I'm always open to some after work, heavy lifting," Keith smiled.

"Are you implying I'm heavy, sir?"

"Not at all. I mean, I like a woman with a little meat on her bones," he lifted slightly to peek at her silhouette. "You'll get no complaints from me."

Alexis nibbled on her bottom lip. Keith's words always had a way of making her spine tingle. Even when she didn't want them to. Gazing down, she fumbled with box contents to hide her flushed expression. She wasn't a shy person by any means, yet he managed to bring that out of her. The more time they spent together, the more he was beginning to dismantle the walls she'd carefully built around her heart.

"Good to know," she said, turning back around to check on the gumbo. Seeing it was nearly done, she grabbed a wine glass from the cabinet. She needed something to relax all the fluttering in her stomach.

"I also have something else for you," he told her.

Alexis popped the cork. "What? You've already bought this expensive bottle of wine," she glanced at him.

Keith held out a card for her, and she reached for it.

"A private detective?"

"Yes, he's a friend of mine. Actually, a friend of my father's. He used to be on the force, but he's retired now and does this on the side. Give him a call; he can probably help you out. I'm sure he still has a few contacts he could reach out to."

Alexis smiled sincerely.

"What?" he asked, noticing her smile.

"I didn't even think about going this route, and here you come with yet another great idea." She sat the bottle down and walked around, stopping in front of him. She kissed his cheek gently. "Thank you, Keith…for everything. I know that I haven't been the best when it comes to you, so I appreciate you being patient with me."

He pushed his cheeks as high as they could go, displaying the charming smile he'd given her the first time they met. She could tell he was proud of himself.

"So does that mean I get another point?"

Pouring her wine, she answered, "A point...a point for what?"

"In the win column. Do I get another point?"

"I can't believe you're keeping tabs," she said, chuckling.

"Oh, I'm most definitely keeping count."

"And what happens when you reach a certain number?"

"I guess we'll find out," he winked, picking up his water.

Alexis peered over the rim of her glass as she sipped her wine. Their eyes were locked on one another as they stared at each other intensely. By the way, he was looking at her and making her feel, she knew exactly how this evening was going to end.

CHAPTER TWENTY

Mathias sat in the back of the diner, waiting for her to show up. He wanted her to see him, see his face the minute she walked in. He was livid at the fact she chose to show up at his house unannounced and with a child, nonetheless. She'd called him a few times, but he hadn't bothered answering. She'd even left messages, but he left them unanswered. Still, if this was what she had to tell him, she could've come to the church.

Instead, she chose to disrupt his household with this unsavory news.

He didn't realize how much chaos she caused until he saw Leslie days ago. The hurt in her eyes, the anger her tone was submerged in; he knew it'd be a long time before they ever got back to the point of happiness. The mistrust she now has for him is beyond comparison. He's never seen her that enraged. She could barely look at him. He never foresaw that moment.

The moment when his betrayal stared him right back in the face.

"Can I get you anything, sir?" the waitress asked.

"Just coffee, please."

"Cream and sugar?"

"Cream is fine," he answered.

She jotted his order down and left to get it. Mathias checked his watch and saw it was 10:15 AM. They agreed to meet at 10:30. He'd come earlier to allow himself some time to collect his thoughts and figure out what he was going to say. He knew he'd be expressing his displeasure with her showing up at his house.

The waitress returned with his coffee, placing it on the table. "Can I get you anything else?" she asked.

"No, this is fine."

She nodded. "Let me know if you need anything."

Mathias smiled as she moved to wait at the other tables. The diner was fairly empty with the exception of the couple sitting a few tables in front of him and a few people at the counter. He picked this place intentionally. It was on the outskirts, far enough for the nosy residents of Deridder. The last thing he wanted was for anyone, especially his church members, to see him with Vanessa. It would give the wrong impression. And he was already in enough hot water.

The bell hanging about the door rang.

A couple of people at the counter peeked over their shoulders and then turned back around. Mathias slowly lifted his head and gazed at her. She looked as tempting as the day he met her. Her figure-eight silhouette was still intact despite her having a child. Her long, brown hair was pinned up in a playful ponytail with a few loose tendrils hanging on the side, adding to her youthful appeal.

Shaking off his wayward thoughts, Mathias waved his hand, signaling where he was sitting. Vanessa sashayed over to where he sat and stood at the edge of the booth. Mathias gave her a blank stare as he waited for her to sit down. He wasn't here for her antics. He had questions that needed answers. Particularly pertaining to the paternity of the child she claimed was his.

Realizing there would be no amorous gestures exchanged, Vanessa eased herself into the booth. She slid her purse strap off her arm and gestured for the waitress, then placed her hands on top of the table and folded them. She said nothing and returned the emotionless gaze he was giving her.

Mathias swallowed. Being this close to her again triggered a stirring in his lower region. He lifted his cup and took a sip, hoping to distract himself from her plunging neckline and enhanced bosom. The dress she had on was not befitting a meeting in a diner, but knowing her, she wore it for that exact reason. Vanessa knew what she was doing. He was certain of that. She was never okay with the fact he chose to stay with Leslie instead of building a life with her. Some of which he was responsible for, considering he'd gotten more involved with her than any of the others.

They didn't part on bad terms, but she wasn't happy about the parting. Still, purposely sabotaging his marriage was inexcusable. He placed the mug down.

"Vanessa," he greeted her.

Her lips curved into a sly grin. She knew why he called her here to the edge of town where no one would see them. He'd done it plenty of times while they were engaged in their indecent affair. Worried about someone from his church recognizing him and possibly running back to his boring wife and telling her house her husband is a fraud.

The waitress came over and Vanessa ordered a tea. Something told her this wouldn't be a long conversation. Pleasant either. Once she walked away, Vanessa glanced back at him.

"Mathias, nice to finally hear from you. Didn't think you'd gotten any of my messages or seen my calls," she said sarcastically. "What do I owe this sudden interest?"

Mathias clenched his jaw. "Cut the crap, Vanessa, you know why I called you. Why would you show up at my house like that? And then feed my wife those lies, knowing that child is not mine? What were you trying to accomplish by doing that?"

The waitress returned with her tea. Pretending she didn't hear what transpired moments before she arrived. It wasn't hard to see that the dynamic between them was strained.

"Is there anything else I can get you?" she asked.

Vanessa shook her head. Mathias did the same. Satisfied, the waitress scurried off back behind the counter. Stirring her tea, Vanessa peered back over at him.

"I wasn't trying to accomplish anything other than this right here. All I wanted to do was talk to you and tell you about Nadia. She's our child, Mathias."

Mathias let out a mocking chuckle. "Vanessa, what's your angle? Because I know you have one. Why did you call me?" he asked again.

"And the reason since we both know Nadia is not mine."

Vanessa glared at him, furious by his unspoken accusation. The sheer audacity that he displayed was outlandish. Accusing her of anything other than what she came here for. She sipped her tea, not taking her eyes off him. "I told you why I came," she stated firmly.

"If that's the case, why didn't you come to the church? Huh? Because we both know you could have. No, you went to my house because you were trying to make a point. You were trying to stir up this mess that you created."

"Mess that I created!" Vanessa slammed her hand down on the table. The porcelain mugs clanked against the table, rattling the silverware with it. "You have the nerve to put this on me when you're the one who cheated on your wife!"

"Yet you knew I was married, and you still slept with me. So what does that say about you, Vanessa?"

"It says I'm a complete idiot for falling in love with a man who is incapable of loving someone other than himself. Be realistic, Mathias, you don't love me or your wife."

Mathias seethed from within. He didn't appreciate her presumptuous thought.

"Now we can either come to terms that you and I can agree with, or I'm going to flounce into your church and tell the entire congregation that you're a fraud and adulterer. What would you like to do?"

Squeezing his fist underneath the table, Mathias silently counted to ten. Vanessa was pushing all of his buttons, and losing his cool in this restaurant, regardless of how far he was, was not ideal. He was still a known pastor, and one video posted on social media would bring loads of unwelcome attention to his doorstep.

"You'd do good not to threaten me," he warned.

"Then it behooves you not to ignore me. We could've had this conversation over the phone, but you kept ignoring my calls."

"Considering you're my mistress, I didn't think communicating with you was a good idea. We broke it off and went our separate ways. Nothing else needed to be said."

"That's all fine and dandy if a child wasn't involved, but she is. Therefore, we need to communicate. You need to meet your daughter."

Mathias shook his head. "I'm not doing this. No, I'm not doing this. I'm not meeting her until we take a paternity test. I will not introduce myself to her until I am sure I'm her father."

Vanessa turned her lip up. She was hurt, but she wouldn't let him see it. She expected some opposition from him since she showed up at his house, but she didn't anticipate the bickering and outright refusal to believe he was the father of her child. But fine, she'd give him what he wanted so they could move forward. She drank the remainder of her tea.

"Fine, I'll call you with the arrangements," she snapped.

Mathias reached into his shirt pocket, pulling out a business card. He slid across the table toward her. "No need, I already made an appointment. The information is on the back. Don't be late. I'd hate to think you were trying to hide something."

Vanessa sneered at him and picked up the card. She slid out of the booth and stood to walk away. There was nothing left for them to say. It was clear he wasn't going to be rational about this. She'd hoped they could talk, maybe walk down memory lane, possibly even rekindle what they once had, but it appeared that wasn't going to happen. Now she had to play hardball. If Mathias wanted to be rivals, she'd be fine with that.

CHAPTER TWENTY-ONE

Grace moved around her room, tossing clothes into her suitcase. She decided to take the job her assistant had emailed her about. As much as she was enjoying her vacation, it was time for her to get back to work. Do something that would take her mind off of everything that had occurred since she'd been here. After her conversation with her mother, she felt like a part of her that had been dismantled felt healed. They'd never apologized for what they did to her, and it hurt that it took losing one parent before either of them did. It also bothered her that her father had apologized months ago, but her stubbornness prevented her from opening the letter.

Perhaps had she done so, they could've talked it out and made peace with one another. Unfortunately, all she'd ever have regarding his last words to her was the letter asking for her forgiveness. He would always tell them, *"Living a life full of regrets is not living at all,"* and she believed him, now more than ever.

Bzzzz. Grace's phone vibrated across the nightstand. When she picked it up, she saw it was a text from her assistant. It was confirmation of her travel arrangements and the details needed for the photoshoot she was doing in New Orleans. She'd hoped it was from Daniel, but he hadn't returned a single text that she'd sent him.

Prior to the conversation with her mother, she was reluctant to accept the job offer; but after careful consideration, she knew it was the universe nudging her in the right direction. Not only that, but it was time. Whether she wanted to admit it or not, Grace was tired. Tired of pretending this gnawing secret and grudge wasn't eating away at her.

She tossed her phone on the bed and went back to packing. She was slated to leave first thing in the morning. The way she set everything up, she'd have a whole day to herself before having to be at the photoshoot. Between the drive there and Daniel working, that'd give her enough time to work up the nerve and figure out how she was going to lay everything out. Her mother had advised her to be straightforward and put everything on the table, but this was a delicate matter that had to be spoon-fed to him.

DING DONG! DING DONG!

Arching her brow, Grace peered over at the clock on the wall and saw it was almost five. She didn't recall her mother saying she was expecting someone, and neither was she. Moving toward the window, she parted the blinds to see if she could figure out who was outside. Her mother had left earlier, so she was here by herself. Glancing out, she spotted the sports car she remembered Mackenzie's husband showing up in.

"What the hell," she mumbled, closing the blinds and storming toward the front. "I know damn well he didn't bring his narrow tail back over here when I told him not to come back."

Grace strolled to the door and flung it open, furious that he had the audacity to show his face again. She was surprised to see him, to say the least, since she figured he'd be long gone by now. Or, at the very least, he would've found Mackenzie. As far as she knew, she was still at Leslie's, and since Leslie was ignoring her calls, she had no way of verifying it. Rose hadn't had much luck either, but she had her stuff going on, so she probably wasn't worried about it or her at the moment.

"Can I help you?" Grace asked snidely. She stood in front of the screen door and crossed her arms aggressively across her chest, staring venomously at him. "I could've sworn I told you *not* to come around here again."

He detected the annoyance in her voice and expressions because his facial expressions projected the same. "I'm looking for Mackenzie. I know she's here. She sent me a message saying she's in Atlanta, but I know she's lying. She's just trying to get me to leave town because you all warned her I was here."

He really is a psychopath, Grace thought. "I don't know what you're talking about."

"The hell you don't!" he shouted. Rage flushed Jasper's face as he scowled at her. He was at his wit's end with Mackenzie and her family. Pulling out his phone, he showed Grace the same picture he sent to Mackenzie. "Now, I already told your sister, and I'm going to tell you. We can do this the easy way or the hard way. Whichever you prefer is fine with me!"

Grace stood frozen as she stared at her mother on his phone. How the hell did he get a picture of her? Was he following her? Has he been following all of them? Questions raced frantically through her head as she tried to keep her cool. She didn't want to give him the satisfaction of thinking he had her rattled. Glaring at him, she smirked at his feeble threat.

"You're following my mother now?" she asked. "I'm calling the police. This is your last time coming here and threatening me and my family."

"Do it, and by the time they get here, they'll find a body, but it won't be mine," he threatened again.

The hairs on the back of Grace's neck stood tall at the finality of his threat. His tone had shifted from sarcastic asshole to full-blown madman. His face too. The longer she stared at him, the more she realized how serious he was. His menacing gaze had barely flinched when he spewed his threat. And his brooding energy was like thick smoke hovering over her. There was something about him, something that told her Mackenzie had made the worst decision of her life.

"Get the hell off our property," she yelled.

"I'm not going anywhere until your sister returns what belongs to me."

"And what might that be? Because my sister doesn't *belong* to you!" Grace told him matter-of-factly.

Jasper scoffed at her brazenness. "You must be the feisty one."

"Feisty…crazy…psychotic…pick one. I'd be more than happy to aid you in your discovery."

"I see where she gets it from," he chucked sinisterly. "But I'm not playing with your sister anymore. Either she returns my money, or she's going to regret the day she met me. So will you. The cop told me he saw her a few days ago with somebody named Carter Reed at some restaurant and then again at the motel. If you think I won't scorch the earth to find her, you're sadly mistaken."

Grace's ears perked up at his mention of Carter and seeing Mackenzie. She assumed she was still at Leslie's cooling off, not hiding out in town with her childhood crush. But that was Mickey. She'd always find someone to help her get out of trouble. She shouldn't have been surprised Carter was the unlucky participant, but she wasn't. Mickey knew he had feelings for her once and probably still did, hence his unknowledgeable walk into the line of fire.

Figuring she could just pay him whatever she took so he could disappear, she asked, "How much did she take? How much will it take for you to leave my sister and our family alone?"

Jasper slowly grazed his finger along his dark goatee. Grace waited for him to give her whatever number he was conjuring up so he could leave. She didn't know how much Mackenzie had stolen, but she guessed it couldn't have been that much.

"Seven hundred and fifty thousand."

"Come again?" she replied.

"Seven hundred and fifty thousand. That's how much of my money your sister stole from me, then ran off."

Instantly Grace knew this situation with him was only the beginning. Mackenzie stealing that much money from anyone put a bounty on her head. She wished she would've just told them she needed money instead of stealing it. Grace swallowed the thick lump that had formed in her throat. As she fought to maintain her composure, she tried to put the pieces together while attempting to reason with how Mackenzie would have stolen that much money. Not to mention where the hell either of them could've gotten it from?

She ran the past few weeks back. Replaying Mackenzie's clandestine behavior and how she'd been jumpy and distant from the moment she'd gotten here. Then there was the mysterious duffel bag she clung to for dear life. Grace hadn't thought much of it at the time, figuring it was full of items of clothing since she showed up unexpectedly like she was on the run. Which, as it turned out, she was. Grace inhaled deeply. Now it all made sense; Mickey showing up in the middle of the night; her not having a phone; him reporting her missing to draw her out, but leaving the missing money detail out, all of it.

The two of them were playing a dangerous game of cat and mouse.

Grace eyed him. He looked like a gloried pimp from what she could see. He wasn't flashy, but his appearance and how he carried himself didn't quite give her businessman. Not the legit kind, anyway. Which would explain why he was looking for her instead of having the police do it. Unless it was ill-gotten, anyone missing that kind of money would have reported it. Then they wouldn't be able to. Nevertheless, it didn't matter. Grace was in no way, shape, form, or fashion about to pay him that kind of money.

"There's nothing I nor my family can do for you. Now again, leave before I call the police," she repeated as she started to close the door.

"Not acceptable," he growled. Determined to prove she was a liar, Jasper flung the screen door open and pushed Grace back, shoving his way inside. Grace slammed hard into the wall behind her as the door nearly hit her face. Proving he was the crazed person Mackenzie probably painted him to be, he rushed through the house.

"Mackenzie! Mackenzie! I know you're in there. You either come out, or your sister will pay your debt!"

Fear coursed through Grace as Jasper's words nearly paralyzed her. She had no idea what he was capable of, nor could she believe he was stomping through her parents' home like he owned the place. Snapping back to reality, Grace patted her pocket to search for her phone when she remembered she left it on the bed. *Crap,* she thought, panicking. She looked around for something—anything she could use to hit him with.

Then it hit her.

Rushing to her father's gun cabinet, Grace quickly pulled out her father's shotgun. She fumbled the box of shells, spilling them onto the floor. "Breath, Grace," she told herself as she bent down to pick them up. Grabbing a couple of shells, she loaded them and snapped the gun back into place, and held it up as she followed the sound of his footsteps. That was one thing her father had taught her. All of them, actually. It'd been a while since she handled a shotgun, but she was glad she had paid attention when she did.

Walking upstairs, she found Jasper shoving doors open, storming in and out of rooms, searching for her sister. Cocking the forearm back, Grace pointed the gun at him. Jasper halted his steps at the sound of the loaded gun. He'd heard that sound enough to know what was pointed at his back.

"You have two seconds to the hell out of my parents' house, or I'm going to make my sister a widow instead of the divorcee she should be," Grace warned.

Holding his hands up, Jasper slowly turned around to face Grace. The condescending scowl plastered on his face told Grace he didn't believe she would use the gun. He stood still, remaining steadfast in finding Mackenzie or, at the very least, his money.

"That's a big gun. You sure you know how to use it?"

Grace glared at him. "You want to find out?"

"All I want is my money," he reminded her.

"And like I said, it's not here. Now unless you want me to put a couple of holes inside of you and bury you out back, I suggest you start walking. Otherwise, you're going to be the one who's a missing person."

Jasper snickered. He was furious, but he was mildly amazed at how she held that gun. It seemed she and Mackenzie were more alike than he anticipated. And if she was anything like

Mackenzie, he knew she would follow through with her threat. Accepting this small feat, Jasper slowly made his way toward Grace.

"Aht…Aht…Aht," she said, "Slowly, that way."

Keeping the gun pointed at him, Grace directed him down the other set of stairs. She was no fool, and she wouldn't let him get close to her and risk him taking the gun from her. Slowly, she followed him downstairs until they reached the front door. Jasper, with his hands still up, stopped in the doorway and then peeked over his shoulders.

"I'm still here," Grace informed him. "Now get the hell out and don't ever come back here."

Frustrated, Jasper flashed her another menacing glare. Then he smirked. "This isn't over. I'm going to find your sister and my money."

Grace didn't say anything else as he pushed the screen door open and walked down the stairs. She watched as he got into his car and turned on to the road. A cloud of dirt followed him as he sped up the road. She slammed the door and rushed to her room to grab her phone. Dialing Leslie's number, she tapped her foot on the floor as she waited for her to answer. Nothing. She dialed again. This time pacing back and forth. The phone rang-and-rang before it went to voicemail again.

"Dammit, Leslie! This is not the time," she yelled into her phone. Trying again, she pressed Leslie's name, hoping she would get the message and answer. After a few seconds, Leslie's pre-recorded voice popped up again. "This girl!"

Of all the times for Leslie to be childish and petty, she picked now. Grace let out a deep breath as she begrudgingly scrolled her contacts to find Mathias's number. She hoped to God it was still the right one since she couldn't recall the last time she dialed it.

She located Mathias's number and tapped it. She pressed the speaker icon on her as it rang.

"Hello," he answered.

Thank God, Grace thought. "Hey, Mathias…this is Grace," she introduced, purposefully saying her actual name. She never cared for him to call her Gigi. "Is my sister with you?"

"Which one?" he asked.

She rolled her eyes. "Seriously? Which sister would I be calling you about? Leslie! Is she with you?" she asked, trying not to sound irritated.

"No, she's not."

"Are you at home?"

"No, I'm not at the house."

Grace craned her neck back, detecting something in his voice. "Umm…well…is she?"

"I'm not sure. I'm not staying at the house right now," he informed her.

Grace groaned at his confession. She wanted to delve deeper into why, but she didn't like him well enough to show any type of concern. Knowing him, he did something, and her sister put him out. She could probably guess what, too. Grace tapped her foot on the hardwood floor. "Okay well, she's not answering my calls, so can you find out where she is? I need to speak with her."

"Mmm hmm, I see. You two must be into again," he pointed out.

"Something like that…."

"Well, she may not answer for me either. Let me call her and see."

"Alright," she said and hung up.

Slipping on some different pants, Grace searched for where she had placed her father's keys while waiting for him to return her call. Since her mother drove her car into town, Grace was left with the pickup truck. She hated that Rose was gone because she'd been here to help her deal with all this madness. She made a mental note to call her the minute she hopped in the truck.

Right when she grabbed her purse, her phone rang again.

"Hello, did you find her?" she rattled off.

"Yes, she's at that place your father left you all to remodel," he replied.

"Thanks."

Grace didn't give him a chance to say anything before she hung up and raced out the door.

CHAPTER TWENTY-TWO

"Code blue! Code blue!" one of the nurses called out. "Room twelve!"

"Get the crash cart," another one yelled.

Alexis hopped up and rushed to the patient room, where the alert was sounding off in. This was her third code blue of the night, and she was beyond exhausted. She hated nights like this, but she understood they came with the job. Some nights were a walk in the park while on others, she earned every dollar they paid her. She, along with two other nurses and Doctor Vaughn, rushed into the room.

"What happened?" Doctor Vaughn asked.

"She was fine a minute ago. I had just checked on her," Alexis told him.

"Lay her back," Doctor Vaughn ordered Lisa, one of the nurses who was in there. Lisa lowered the bed and moved the pillow from beneath the patient's head. "Let's start compressions."

Alexis started CPR as they readied the defibrillator. "One…two…three," Alexis counted out as Lisa squeezed the resuscitation bag. They both looked at the monitors and saw there was no change in rhythm. "Again," Alexis said, continuing compressions, alternating with Lisa pumping the bag. When nothing changed, Doctor Vaughn intervened.

"Okay, step back," he said, grabbing the defibrillator pads. He placed them on each side of the patient's chest. "Charge it to two hundred."

"Charged," Alexis called out.

"Now!" he commanded.

Alexis pressed the button, and the patient's body jolted, showing no signs of a pulse. The green line remained flat, and she put her finger on the button as she readied herself to increase the voltage. Doctor Vaughn waited only seconds before giving the order again.

Doctor Vaughn commanded, "Charge it to two-seventy-five."

Alexis pressed the arrow to increase the voltage. "Ready," she called out.

"Now!" he ordered.

Pressing the button again, everyone stood watch to see if there would be any changes, and when there weren't any, Doctor Vaughn ordered her to increase the voltage two more times. Alexis exhaled deeply between each breath to slow her heart rate down.

"Restarting chest compressions," Doctor Vaughn said, placing his hand on the patient's chest.

For the next six minutes, he alternated between chest compressions and the oxygen bag. When the patient presented no changes, he called it.

"Time of death, 4:30 AM. Great job, everyone," Doctor Vaughn told them, although no one felt that way. Still, they gave their all, and the doctors never wanted their efforts to go unnoticed or unrecognized.

Alexis took another deep breath as she moved to exit the room so housekeeping and the techs could clean the room, and the morgue staff could prepare the patient to be moved to the morgue. Another death. Another family had to be notified of the loss of their loved one. She was exhausted—physically and emotionally. This was her second patient that died tonight, and all she wanted was to finish the next hour-and-a-half of her shift sans another cardiac arrest or death.

"Are you okay?" Lisa asked as they walked back to the nurse's station.

Alexis nodded even though she wasn't. Normally, she wouldn't be *this* affected since, after six years, she'd gotten accustomed to these types of nights. However, with all that she had going on personally, tonight weighed on her.

"I'm going to grab some coffee from the cafeteria," Alexis told her. "Can you watch everything until I get back?"

"Yeah, girl, I got you," Lisa answered.

Alexis smiled. "Thanks. Did you want one?"

Lisa rattled off her order. "Sure, black...decaf...two sugars."

"Got it," Alexis said. She reached inside her pocket to make sure her pager was there and headed to the café. She was in dire need of some caffeine. Anything to boost her energy because she was running on empty. As she stood in front of the elevator, she felt her phone buzz. Pulling it out, Alexis saw it was an email from the PI Keith had recommended. After he gave her the information, she called him right away. Since her search for her birth certificate was a failed effort, she pivoted, figuring he could work in conjunction with the test she mailed off.

Stepping off the elevator, Alexis walked down the hallway. "Wow, that was quick," she said, reading the email he'd sent. Inside, it contained Daniel's information and his whereabouts. "He's a doctor."

"Who's a doctor?" Keith asked from behind her.

Alexis spun around. "My father. My biological father," she corrected. "Your contact was able to locate him, and he sent me the information."

Keith smiled. "I told you he could help you."

"You did. I guess I didn't expect him to locate him this quick."

Alexis stared at the information. Now that she had it, she felt on edge about reaching out. What would he say? What would she say? There were so many questions and thoughts racing through her mind. Keith placed his hand on her forearm, and somehow that calmed her.

"It's going to be okay," he assured her.

She nodded. "Thanks."

"So, he's a doctor too? Guess that explains your attraction to doctors and your interest in medicine," he teased.

Alexis playfully shoved him and giggled. "That'd be a little odd, don't you think?"

"Not really. You know they always say, 'girls date their fathers, and boy marry their mothers.' Clearly, that's true in your case."

He has a point, Alexis thought as she filled her cup with coffee and then Lisa. She had to give it to Grace, despite her poor efforts in parenting, she at least didn't procreate with a dummy.

"What are you thinking?" Keith asked, cutting through her thoughts.

"I was just thinking about how at least Grace chose someone that was intelligent to conceive a child with. God knows I would be even more terrified if she chose a bum."

Keith laughed.

"You're laughing, but I'm serious. Ever since I found out, I've been trying to figure out what he's like, what he's done with his life, everything. I thought he'd be some artsy type like Grace, but as it turns out—he's into more logical, analytical things."

"Watch it now. You almost sound like a proud daughter."

Alexis frowned. "Far from it. Let's not forget he willingly signed away his responsibility, just like Grace. Proud is not even close to what I feel about him."

They walked up to the cashier, and Keith paid for their coffee. Alexis remembered she didn't grab Lisa's sugars and circled back to get them. Tucking them in her pocket, she rejoined Keith, and they headed back to their perspective places.

"Okay well, don't keep me in suspense; what did he send you?" he asked her.

She glanced over at him. "Everything. His phone number, address, where his practices are located…you name it."

"Practices?" Keith repeated.

"Yes, practices. He has one in Deridder and another in New Orleans."

"Wow! That's awesome. What's his specialty?"

"General Medicine," she answered.

Keith nodded, impressed. "Let's call him. Right now."

"Keith, it's five o'clock in the morning. Don't you think that's insane? What am I supposed to say? Hi, I'm Alexis; sorry to wake you, but I just wanted to call you and let you know I'm the child you threw away."

Keith stopped to face her. "I wouldn't suggest that introduction," he laughed. "I'd go with a simple greeting, then tell him who you are and why you're calling. I'm sure he would respond a little better to that."

"I don't know, Keith. All of this feels weird. I don't even know if he knows about me."

"How can he not? He does know he has a child out there somewhere."

"True, but I mean, I'm not sure he knows that his long-lost child is the alleged little sister of his high school sweetheart. I mean, I was literally in the same town as him, and he had no clue."

"You don't think Grace told him yet? You said she wanted to tell him first, then you, right?"

"Right, but that doesn't mean she did," Alexis replied. "I know, Grace. She's always done things in her own time. Hence me not knowing, or probably ever knowing, she was my mother. I don't know why all of a sudden, I feel this might not be a good idea. What if he flips out? Better yet, what if he rejects me? What if he is perfectly fine not knowing me or anything about me?"

Keith placed his free hand on Lexi's again. He could see she was spiraling and overthinking. She tended to do that when she felt like she was losing control. Stepping forward, he placed a soft kiss on her cheek then he stepped back. He knew how Lexi felt about their co-workers knowing about their relationship. Her past experiences

"First, calm down. Secondly, you are a phenomenal woman who anyone would be happy to claim as their child, but in the event, he doesn't— you did what you set out to do…find your father. We have no control over how anyone responds, so keep that in mind. Now, I'm here, and I'll be here whenever you are ready to call him. You don't have to do this alone, Lexi. Remember that."

Alexis almost teared up at his words of comfort. He saw right through her, and that was something she had never experienced before. Even with Quinn, he never got her as Keith does. She was beginning to see that more and more.

"Thank you, Keith. I appreciate that."

CHAPTER TWENTY-THREE

Leslie looked around the courtyard, taking in the splendor of the grounds, when her phone buzzed against her thigh. She was waiting for the appraiser to show up. Pulling it out, she saw Grace's name appear on her screen. She was calling again. Leslie rolled her eyes. She'd been ignoring her calls since their last blowout. "Not today, Satan," she said, pressing the decline button.

She'd come close to calling a couple of times then opted not to for the simple fact that's what Grace expected her to do. Leslie was tired of being the bigger person all the time. Not to mention, all of them tended to do that when it came to Grace, and she was tired of it.

She slid her phone back into her purse when it vibrated again. "Dear God, Gigi!" Glancing at it, she saw this time it was Mathias calling. Not wanting to speak to him either, she hesitated. Their last conversation didn't end well at all, and if it weren't for him having their children, she wouldn't answer him either.

"Hello."

"Leslie…"

"What, Mathias? What do you want now?"

"I wanted to talk about us."

Figures. Leslie rolled her eyes. He'd already called to ask where she was, claiming Grace was looking for her; now he wanted to talk about *them*. She wasn't in the mood for this right now.

"I wanted to let you know that I'm handling everything in regard to Vanessa. I'm doing what I can to fix this."

Leslie grunted. "Okay, and?"

"What does that even mean?"

"It means I don't care, Mathias. You rushing to get a test, thinking that's the band-aid to put on your catastrophic behavior, is beyond astounding. Whether she's yours or not, the fact she could've been is the real problem. She's the outcome of what you did, not the root of it. How do you not see that?"

"I do, Leslie. I'm just grasping straws right now. Doing whatever I can to show you I don't want what we have to end."

"It was over the first time you cheated, and I was too stupid to see that. I should have never married you. When I caught you before Myles and then again before Micah, I should've known then you wouldn't do right, but I convinced myself that you proposing to you were you seeing the error of your ways. Clearly, I was wrong. Once a cheater, always a cheater."

"That's how you feel about us?" he asked.

Leslie heard the hurt in his tone, but she didn't care one iota. She'd given Mathias a chance after chance, and each time, he managed to mess it up worse than the time before. It was time she started looking out for self, and it started cleaning her own house.

"That's exactly how I feel about us, now…if there's nothing else, I'd like to get back to doing what I am doing," she said dismissively.

"Eighteen years…" he murmured.

"Spare me. You didn't care about the time spent together when you pulled your pants down and penetrated four different women, so neither did it. Somethings and some people are meant to be history."

There was a slight pause. She squeezed her temple. That's why she didn't want to tell him. Leslie knew he wasn't fully onboard with her plans because they didn't include him. He liked knowing she was home, tucked away inside while he did whatever he wanted to do with whomever. With him being out of the house, Leslie had time to assess their marriage, realizing how one-sided it had been. They held the phone while they waited for the other to say something.

"I scheduled a session with Pastor Brooks," he told her. It was his last-ditch effort to fix his marriage. He was certain that Vanessa's child wasn't his and this way she could see how serious he was.

"Cancel it," she said coldly. "Is there isn't anything else?"

Mathias cleared his throat at the same time she heard the door close. Curious as to who it might've been, Leslie walked into the hallway.

"Hello," he called out.

"Leslie…who is that?" Mathias asked, clearly hearing the masculine voice.

"Hi, can I help you?" she asked, ignoring Mathias's questioning.

Mathias started rambling in her ear, so she eased it down to her side so she could hear what the stranger was going to say. Staring down at him, Leslie tried to pinpoint who he was, but she'd never seen him before. Most people here, she knew. Therefore, when unfamiliar faces came into town, they weren't hard to spot.

He grinned politely. "Yes, I'm looking for Ernest Bayou..".".

"And you are?"

"My name is Levi Cunningham. Do you know where I can find him?"

She'd never heard that name before or recalled her uncle mentioning it. Raising the phone back up to her ear, Leslie heard Mathias still talking.

"Let me call you back," she said, then hung up.

"How can I help you?" she repeated. "Are you the appraiser?"

He laughed off her slight insult. Levi didn't know what appraisers looked like but he certainly felt he didn't look like one. "Yes, I was looking for Ernest Bayou. I was told he was the owner of this property."

"Told by who exactly?" she questioned.

"Okay, you got me. I found his information through public records," he admitted.

Leslie quirked her brow. "Obviously, you didn't do your due diligence," she subliminally replied.

"I'm not sure I follow," he answered.

"That much is obvious. May I ask why you were doing a public search on this property?"

"I'd think that'd be something I speak with Mr. Bayou about," he countered, not wanting to speak with anyone who wouldn't be of use to him. He was on a tight schedule, and if he wanted to get those government contracts, he needed to speed things up.

"He's not available at the moment. And I'm not sure he will be for quite some time. However, I'm his daughter, Leslie. I'm sure I can be of some assistance to you."

Levi contemplated his response. She appeared to be the second daughter he'd met, assuming the one he met in the diner awhile back was actually one of his daughters and not a relative, but he wasn't able to really find out anything thanks to the two women who barged in and interrupted them.

Now as he stood here talking to her, he wasn't sold on the fact she'd be any easier to talk to, though he'd still try. Levi reached into his pocket to retrieve one of his business cards.

Handing it to her, Leslie glanced down at the name on the card, *Ambrose Properties*. Beneath it was his name, as he stated, with property development listed underneath it. Between the heaviness of the material and the embossed gold lettering, the card looked and felt expensive.

"Property development," Leslie uttered. "What's a property development company looking into this property for?"

"We have some ideas in mind," he answered vaguely.

"Such as?"

"I think that's something I'd like to discuss with Mr. Bayou."

Fed up with his ambiguity, Leslie replied, "Mr. Bayou is no longer with us, and you are talking to one of the owners. What is it that you're here to inquire about?"

"I'd like to make him…I mean…you, an offer to purchase the property."

"An offer? What kind of an offer? And who said this property was for sale?"

"No one, but I figured once I made you a generous offer, you'd be happy to sell."

"That's pretty arrogant of you to think that when there is nothing to indicate we are selling."

"I think once you see this number, you'll change your mind." He extended the offer to Leslie, and she stared at it before accepting it. "I'm sure that amount is well above what you would actually receive for this place."

Unfolding the paper, Leslie stared at the number in front of her, shocked by what he'd presented. Glancing back at him, she said, "Thank you for this offer, but it's not for sale."

"I'm sorry, maybe you didn't look at the number I offered."

"I'm well aware of what you offered, but as I stated—it's not for sale."

Levi narrowed his eyes, stunned by her refusal. He'd just offered her millions and by the looks of this town, and everyone in it; no one was equipped with that kind of cash.

"Everything is for sale," he stated plainly.

"Maybe where you're from, but around here, that isn't the case. Now if you'll excuse me—" she stretched out her hand, ushering him toward the door— "I'm about to lock up. It was nice meeting you, Mr. Cunningham."

Easing over to the door, he stopped right as he placed his hands on the knob and turned around.

"Is there something else?" Leslie asked.

"The offer… it won't be on the table long. I'll give you forty-eight hours to reconsider."

Astonished by his continued dismissing what she said, Leslie shook her head. "Thank you for coming out here. I hope it wasn't too much of an inconvenience for you."

He gazed back at her. Remembering something she said. "I'm sorry, you said *we* weren't selling. Who did you mean when you said we?"

Leslie glared at him. "No one you need to concern yourself with. Have a good day."

He grinned. It seemed he needed to step up his due diligence and do a little more digging. He hadn't realized the property had exchanged hands since it was only about a month ago he'd been made aware of who the owner was. That was the only reason he was here. Levi valued speaking to people face-to-face when making them an offer they couldn't refuse; however, in this case, that didn't seem to work. So moving forward, he'd have to figure out who all the players were so he could get what he needed and move on. If she wasn't the only owner, that meant there was another pressure point he could push. Giving him another angle to work.

"You'll be seeing me again, Miss Bayou," he informed her, then closed the door.

"I don't doubt that," she uttered.

Leslie walked over to the door to watch him get into his car through the glass. As he drove off, she reached inside her pocket and grabbed the paper he'd given her. She stared at it again. *Sixteen million dollars,* she thought. That was a lot of money… a lot! Though as tempting as it was, it only inspired her.

Admittedly, if she could get offered this much and they hadn't even renovated it, there was no telling how much she would make by simply hosting events here. They could generate that kind of revenue in five years if they followed her plan. Leslie's eyes sparkled. His offer was a drop in the bucket compared to what she dreamt of leaving her children and her grandchildren. He didn't realize it, but his offer gave her just the motivation she needed.

CHAPTER TWENTY-FOUR

Grace sped up the tree-lined pathway leading up to the enormous estate. She had to admit, this view was beautiful, and the way the sunset shadowed over large trees, forming these pockets of light, seemed almost enchanting. From a photographer's standpoint, the scenery was picturesque and would make for a beautiful backdrop. Despite her reservations about keeping it, she couldn't deny how tranquil the atmosphere felt. As she got closer, she saw a car she didn't recognize and an unfamiliar man climbing inside of it.

Grace inched her car around the circle driveway, and the driver of the other vehicle drove off. Shifting her car into park, Grace turned off the ignition and hopped out of the car. Was this the reason Leslie's been dodging her calls all morning?

She pushed open the door.

"Gigi!" Leslie quickly stuffed the paper inside her pocket. "What are you doing here?"

Grace eyed her little sister. She'd seen her quickly slide a slip of paper in her pocket.

Grace arched her brow. "So that's what you're doing now? Cheating on Mathias? Who was that man?"

Leslie snickered under her breath. "Grace, please, that was someone looking for our father. For your information, I would never cheat on my husband. Worry about your own mess."

Grace rolled her eyes. "Whatever. I wish you'd answer your phone when I called. I think Mickey's in trouble." Leslie glanced around the room before her eyes settled on Grace again. She knew some of what Mickey had going on but wanted to see what Grace was talking about first. "What do you mean she's in trouble?"

She listened as Grace told her about a man who not only claimed to be Mickey's husband but he'd also accused her of stealing a huge sum of money from him. On top of all that, he'd threatened their mother.

Leslie stood stunned. There was no way she heard Grace say Mackenzie's husband threatened their mother. "What do you mean he threatened Mama and barged into the house? What did he say?"

"Apparently, he'd been following Mama, thinking he was going to catch up with Mickey, but when that didn't pan out, he was reduced to coming back to the house upset. Claiming we warned her and was helping her hide out from us. Honestly, I'm not sure if he wants her or the money, he claims she stole from him."

Leslie heard everything Grace was saying, but she couldn't get past the part where he'd threatened their mother or pushed his way into their house. What had Mackenzie gotten herself into? Not to mention she was pregnant by him.

"So, how did you get him to leave? Did you call the police? "

"No, I handled it. I grabbed Daddy's shotgun and ushered him out with that."

Leslie wanted to laugh but she held it. Out of all of them, Grace was the best shot, so the fact he made it out unscathed and alive was a good thing because she certainly wouldn't have missed. On the other hand, Mackenzie had left out quite a bit regarding her runaway bride story. Mainly the part where she robbed the man and took off.

"I'm glad you didn't get hurt."

Grace snickered. "I think you should've been more worried about him."

"That's true, but still...he could've done anything to you before you had a chance to grab the gun. The outcome ended up being in your favor, but we both know with someone that emboldened and enraged, it could've gone differently."

Grace nodded, agreeing with her. "Well, is she at your house? The last time we communicated, she didn't say where she was when I asked. But then, Jasper mentioned a cop told him she was seen in town with Carter at some restaurant and a motel?"

Leslie shrugged. "I haven't talked to Mickey since she left my house, but that was days ago. I assumed she went back to the house. Her being in town doesn't sound too far off-base."

Grace exhaled. Mackenzie and her drama were becoming a nuisance. She had her own issues to attend to. She was at her wit's end trying to find her. It was evident she wanted to be left to her own devices.

"Did you know he was hitting on her?" Grace asked.

"Excuse me?"

"Mickey told me he'd been hitting her for the past two years. Did you know?"

"What kind of question is that, Gigi? Of course, I didn't know. If I did, I wouldn't be standing here shocked about why she's ducking and dodging him. Be for real."

"Then where the hell is she?"

"Where...I don't know. But knowing her, she's probably back in Georgia."

Grace huffed. "You're not going to ask how much she took?"

Leslie shook her head. "No, because I really couldn't care less. I love Mickey, but we both know she makes questionable decisions and then has to solicit help later on. I'm more concerned about the threats he's made and her safety. If he's chasing her for money instead of reporting it stolen, there's a reason for it.

"Can you at least call her and relay the message? I'm not going to keep calling her."

"Do I have a choice? Her husband has threatened our mother. I can try," Leslie said.

"Fine," Grace said, leaning on the wall. "Now, are you going to tell me who that man who left is?

"Some developer," she answered. "But as I said before, nothing to worry about."

"Does he have something to do with that paper you tucked in your pocket?"

"He does, but can you just give me a little more time to get everything together."

"Get what together? I thought we said we were selling?"

"No, you said you wanted to sell. That wasn't everyone's final decision. Besides, it's three to two right now."

"Leslie," Grace began to say but was halted by Leslie raising her hand.

"Gigi...please. For once, can everything not revolve around you?"

Offended, Grace asked, "And what is that supposed to mean?"

"It means everything always has to be on your terms, so the rest of us have to sit on the sidelines until you're ready. It's been that way since we were kids. And I get it, you're the oldest, and somehow, you feel you have to always be in charge, but you don't have to. If you don't want to be a part of this...fine. But don't force everyone else to fall in line with your choices."

"Why are you so defensive? All I asked was who he was?"

"No, you're asking more than that. Don't insult my intelligence, Gigi."

"I'm not insulting your intelligence I want you to look around and see how much of an enormous undertaking this is and think about it," Grace turned around. "And then think about what else we could do individually if we sold this."

Leslie huffed loudly. "Jesus Christ, Gigi! Is there any chance you could just for once see me as something other than a housewife and a mother? I know I didn't finish college like all of you, but that doesn't mean I'm void of ideas and abilities. Nor does it mean I'm incapable of running this place efficiently. Whether you all know it or not, that church's success is me...*Me*!" she pointed to herself, "I am the person who kept that place moving like a well-oiled machine for years. And believe it or not, marriage and taking children are not for the faint at heart. It's work, but you wouldn't know anything about that would you?"

Leslie realized the cheap shot she'd taken when it left her lips, but she was over it and Grace.

She was tired of feeling like she was useless or some kind of dumb blonde, only good for cooking and cleaning. She had no idea the amount of mental strength, along with physical and emotional strength, it took to be present for a house full of people with a million different personalities.

Grace sat her purse down. "Okay, Leslie, let's clear the air." She leaned against the old island. "We've been doing this for over twenty years, and I'm tired. I'm tired of us fighting arguing, and fighting some more. The round-and-round, back and forth—it's exhausting. So, please…say what you need to say."

"What do you think I want to say to you?" Leslie asked.

"I don't know; tell me how upset you are at me for abandoning Lexi. Tell me how you resent the fact that I was able to have a child and move on with my life and have a career while you were here, raising yours. Yell at me for something, but for the love of God, just say it already! Because there's something about me that bothers you because you only have an issue with me."

Leslie placed her hand on her hip. "Fine, you want to know what my issue is, Gigi, I'll tell you. You literally left. You pretended that we didn't exist for years because you wanted to act as if what Mama and Daddy made you do was a cardinal sin. And yes—" Leslie's voice cracked, as she tried not to cry— "there might be a little resentment because of the way you handled things, and then every time you come home, you walk around with this invisible hazard suit on like you want to keep us at a distance. I resent you because your sour feelings toward our parents rubbed off on us."

"That's BS and you know it. I never blamed you or treated you differently, that was you! You started treating me like I was to blame for *you* getting pregnant and not finishing school. And if we're being honest, that's when it started. Your misplaced anger was directed at me when it should've been pointed at you."

"Wow!"

"No, don't do that. Don't act as if I'm attacking you. We both know it's the truth. You've always treated what you clearly felt was a mistake like it was my fault."

"My children aren't mistakes."

"And I'm not saying they are, but you've been acting like they are. You're the only one who's been harboring these feelings when they're your choices. I didn't have a choice. Mine was taken away from me. Did you forget that I was forced to give up my child? Leslie, you willingly made the decision to keep yours when you didn't have to, so stop treating me like a leper because you didn't have the guts to chase your dreams."

"Well…glad to know how you really feel about me," she replied, getting choked up. Leslie wiped her bottom lids.

"Leslie," Grace said softly.

"No, no, Gigi. You've spoken your truth, don't apologize for it."

"I hadn't planned on it." Grace took a long, deep breath. She contemplated her next words.

They were headed in the same direction as always, and that's not what she came here for. She'd come here to see if she knew where Mackenzie was so she could talk some sense into her.

"That clears things up."

"Leslie, I'm sorry. I'm sorry you feel that my leaving somehow affected you, Mama, and Daddy, but did you ever think about what staying might've done to me? I know you were a kid when everything happened, but now that you aren't, put yourself in my shoes for a second. Imagine how I felt for nearly two years having to live in a house with my child, one who I'm not allowed to acknowledge, while my parents raised her as their own. While in some alternate universe, they thought doing so would be a better option, so we'd keep 'the family' together. Think about how that made me feel." Grace roughly swiped her cheek. "Between the lies I was telling myself, the lies I continuously told Daniel, I was suffocating in that house. So I left."

Leslie held her breath at Grace's confession, but then she was over her woe is me—melodrama—everyone feels sorry for me routine. It was exhausting, and the fact all she could focus on was the negative; Leslie had reached her limit.

"How do you think you'd feel if you were in my position?" Grace continued. "As a mother, could you ever see yourself residing with your child every day, but she didn't know you were her mother? Then imagine having to see your first love day in and out, and he's comforting you and trying to be supportive of both you and his situation, but you're lying to him. To keep our family secret, I had to deceive him. That's why I ran. I ran because, as long as I was here, I would have been reminded of the lie. And I was scared that I wouldn't be able to do that for too long, so I went as far as I could and became someone else."

"You know, Gigi," she said, gearing up, "The fact you can't see how fortunate you were is upsetting."

"Wh—"

"Aht…" Leslie held up her finger to cut her off. "Let me finish because I'm tired, and if I had to guess, so is everyone else. They have too much going on to tell you, but I'm going to do everyone, including myself, a favor. Do you know how many children end up in the system—never to be given a chance to know a single person in their family? Do you have a single idea as to how blessed you were to still be able to see and interact with your child even though you squandered it by staying away? You're selfish, and nobody's going to tell you that because they're too busy tiptoeing around your feelings, but time's up." Leslie took a deep breath. "Gigi, grow up. You love to remind us how you're the oldest, yet you don't act like it. You're a grown woman. And you've been given a second chance to build a relationship with Alexis, but like I said— you're selfish and self-centered. You're too busy placating your own feelings and worried about how *Daniel's* going to take the news…who gives a damn?!"

Grace winced as she remained silent while Leslie unloaded on her.

"I'm tired, Gigi," Leslie sighed heavily. "I have four kids, and a husband I'm on the verge of killing while trying to figure out what I want to do with my *own* life, and you think I have time to sit here and keep listening to you whine about Mama and Daddy forcing you to do something we all know you were nowhere near ready to. Take it from me; motherhood is not easy. I was a college student and had to drop out twice...*twice!* All because raising kids *and* finishing school was hard as hell. Meanwhile, you were given the opportunity to go to school and finish. Have you ever stopped and thought about how I wasn't given that same opportunity? I didn't have my parents raising my children so I could chase my dreams. But you did. And you have the audacity to stand here and complain about it. You're ungrateful!"

There was a long moment of silence as they absorbed what was said. As a mother, Leslie understood wholly what Grace felt, even though she never had to make that kind of decision. Their parents hadn't been thrilled when she told them she was pregnant with Myles, only to turn around and tell them less than two years later she was pregnant with Micah. They were livid, actually, which ultimately led to Leslie agreeing to marry Mathias. But Grace was right; those were her decisions. Still, Grace's ungratefulness was suffocating.

"I never thought about it like that," Grace admitted. "But you're right; I was able to make go to college and finish then pursue my career."

Leslie stared at her, expressionless. Grace's epiphany was admirable, but she had no intentions of coddling her anymore. Not that she ever did, but Grace needed to heal whatever broken pieces she had inside of her and stop taking it out on everyone else.

"I'm sorry," Grace apologized. "I'm sorry for punishing you for my decisions because I felt trapped inside this life I created for myself."

Leslie nodded. "I'm sorry too. I could've handled things between us better. Instead, I only added to the hostility and strain, so for that, I'm sorry," Leslie smiled faintly as she walked over to Grace and embraced her. "Truce," Leslie stated.

"Truce."

They held each other for a few minutes and Grace breathed a sigh of relief. She was happy they could finally call a truce and put all of this behind them. The different battles on all fronts were too much to manage anymore.

"Have you talked to Lexi," Leslie asked, stepping back.

"No, I wanted to tell Daniel first."

"And why haven't you told him? I heard the two of you went out, did you tell him then?"

"Yes, I did."

Leslie paused, stunned that she had. She had expected her to say no because after talking to Mackenzie, she figured Grace wouldn't budge on saying anything it just came out.

"Shocker," she said sarcastically. "How'd he take it?"

"Not well. He drove off and he won't return my calls."

"Guess you can finally tell Alexis now, huh."

"Yes. I don't know if it should be over the phone or in person."

"Depends. Knowing Lexi, she's probably not going to answer, so you may have to pay her a surprise visit. Good luck with that. Whatever you choose, you need to make this right," Leslie advised. She would leave out the part where Alexis already knew his name. They'd called a truce, and that would for sure reverse everything.

"I'm going to go see her once I get back from this job in New Orleans if she doesn't answer when I call again."

"The sooner, the better," Leslie encouraged.

"Lexi is never going to forgive me," Grace expressed.

"I will agree she is as stubborn as you, but she will forgive you. Give her some time, but for the love of God, tell her what she needs to know."

Grace pulled her keys out. She had to get some rest before she left for New Orleans. She couldn't wait to get back to California. This was enough drama for a lifetime. "I'm headed to New Orleans tomorrow. If Mickey answers, let her know her husband is hot on her trail, and if she doesn't return that money, we just might be attending another funeral."

"I will do that," Leslie told her. "Oh, and Gigi, I was serious when I said I wanted to take this on. I need you to give me a chance. At least hear me out, and if you still feel like it's something you don't want to do; I'd like to buy your portion."

"Leslie, do you honestly feel this is a good time to take on a venture like this? With all this chaos going on, you want to embark on this journey…this one?"

"Actually, it's keeping me busy, so I'm not sulking over everything."

Grace gave her a peculiar look. She'd picked up on Leslie's subliminal remarks, not to mention the tidbits of information Mathias had made her privy to.

You and Mathias? He mentioned he wasn't staying at the house when I called him looking for you. And you mentioned you were trying not to kill him. What's up with that?"

Leslie shook her head. "No, not right now. Later, maybe. After I've thought everything through."

"Okay, I'll respect that."

Embracing one another again, Leslie whispered, "It's going to be okay, you know. All of this. I wholeheartedly believe Daddy knew what he was doing when he put all this in motion."

Grace silently agreed with her. She had to admit, a part of her had thought the same thing. With him getting older, she felt he wanted things to be right before he left this place. She just never expected it would happen after he left. Or ever, for that matter.

Stepping back, Grace said, "I hope so."

CHAPTER TWENTY-FIVE

Mackenzie made her way to the kitchen, her slippers making a dragging sound against the tile. She'd awakened to a text from Leslie giving her heads up that Grace was frantic at the fact Jasper had stopped by her parents' house once again looking for her. She checked in with her mother only to find out Grace had told her everything and that she'd pulled a gun on Jasper. Mackenzie knew that would only fuel his anger. It seemed he didn't believe her when she told him she was back in Georgia.

Once she finished her tasks for the day, she would call her mother to check on her. Mackenzie knew she was due for a tongue-lashing, but her mother would be the only person she'd accept it from. Especially since Grace had her own issues to deal with. Mackenzie started the coffeemaker when she heard her phone ring. Rushing back to the bedroom, she grabbed her phone off the bed.

"Hey, Lexi," she answered.

"I'm glad to know you made it," Alexis playfully scolded.

"I'm sorry, I meant to call. I've been handling some things since I made it to Atlanta, and I still have a ton of other things to take care of."

"That's all fine and dandy, but a simple text would have sufficed."

"You're right, I apologize. I didn't mean to make you worry," Mackenzie conceded.

"Have you told anybody else you're there?"

"No, and I don't plan to. Speaking of which, girl, why did Leslie text me saying he popped up at our parent's house again."

"Have you called Mama?"

Mackenzie shook her head as if Alexis could see her. "No, not yet. I'm kind of avoiding that conversation."

"Mickey!" Alexis shouted.

"Calm down, Lexi. I already know what you're going to say and before you say it; I'm handling it."

"Are you really? Because it sounds like he's escalating."

"That's an understatement," Mackenzie mumbled under her breath. She'd follow her first mind and exclude the part where he sent a not-so-subtle threat since it would only cause her to panic some more. "However, that'll all be over soon."

"I hope so. How's the little one doing?"

Mackenzie rubbed her hand over her stomach. Most days, she had to remind herself she was carrying a life inside of her. She guessed it hadn't hit her yet. With everything going on with Jasper, relishing becoming a mother seemed like a luxury she couldn't afford yet, and she hated that. Thankfully, her nausea was hit or miss, and the other pregnancy symptoms Leslie warned her about hadn't taken effect just yet.

"We're okay," she said, smiling softly.

"Remember what I told you. Make sure you find a doctor sooner rather than later. Regina fitting you it was just a favor to me. You're under a lot of stress, so you need to be monitored. Especially in this first trimester."

"It's on my list of things to do," Mackenzie admitted. She had a few things to take care of now that she was back; however, her first stop was her house. Since Jasper wasn't here, she'd sneak in and out, and he'd be none the wiser. One thing she did check last night was to see if the password to their security system had been changed. Of course, it wasn't, but that didn't surprise her. Arrogance had always been his Achilles heel at least when it came to her, anyway.

"What else do you have planned?"

Mackenzie replied, "Bank then-attorney," purposefully leaving her detour to their house out. It would only worry Alexis, which in turn she would worry her. "Afterwards, I'll look into the doctors you looked up for me to see who's accepting new patients."

"When are you going to call him?"

Mackenzie paused. She'd asked herself that question a million times already. Each time ending with no time soon. They were past civil conversation at this point. And considering she's siphoned quite a bit of money from him, he wouldn't have a calm bone in his body.

"Honestly, Lexi, I think it's better we only talk through our attorneys at this point."

"Are you ready for this? Because I presume you know this won't be a walk in the park," Alexis told her.

"As ready as I'm going to be."

"How long are you going to stay there?" she asked, referring to her staying in the Airbnb.

"That's on my list of things to do too. I've looked up a few apartment complexes, so I'm going to spend a day viewing them."

"What about your house? Isn't that in both of your names?" Alexis asked.

"No, just his."

"Oh, so guess that means he'll get the house then."

He can have it, Mackenzie thought. These past two years inside of it has been a nightmare, so the last thing she wanted was to live in constant memory of them.

"Not exactly, but I'm not going to fight him on it. The quicker we can finalize this divorce, the better." Mackenzie glanced at the microwave to check the time. It was 10:30 AM. She wanted to get to her house and to the bank before it got too late. Her appointment at the divorce attorney's office was later this afternoon. She'd already done the leg work regarding that, so the rest would be handled once she got there. "But let me get off this phone. I want to run these errands and get back."

"Alright, I'm headed into work anyway. I'll check on you later."

They said their goodbyes and hung up.

Mackenzie grabbed a mug out of the cabinet, poured herself a cup of coffee, and headed toward the shower. She wanted to be back before the sun went down since that's when the devil usually came out to play.

****

Mackenzie sat in the lobby as she waited to be seen. It seemed like sitting in lobbies was her new thing, but she would do whatever she needed to do to get her life back. She managed to sneak into her house undetected to get what she needed and out. She didn't trust that Jasper was still in Deridder. After his stunt at her parent's house, he could've reconsidered what she said and got back on the road. Knowing this, the last thing she wanted to do was leave anything to chance.

She'd already gone to two different banks to put the money in a safe deposit box. That was until she was about to properly disperse and invest it. Mackenzie knew she was going to need somewhere to stay and a new vehicle since she had neither. The Maserati truck she once had was a lost cause. Jasper had put it in her name, but she didn't want to risk him having any holds on her. All she wanted was her business and for her baby to grow up in a healthy, safe environment—far away from him.

"Miss Vincent," the receptionist said.

Mackenzie looked up, cringing at the salutation. It wouldn't be long before she'd be able to rid herself of it. "Yes," she answered.

"Mr. Graham is ready to see you. If you will follow me," she instructed.

Mackenzie stood and followed her to an office door a few doors from the lobby area. "Thank you," she said, walking in.

"You're welcome. Can I get you anything? Another water? Some coffee, perhaps?"

Mackenzie groaned softly. A cup of coffee sounded wonderful right now, but the doctor had advised her to eliminate it from her diet. This kid wasn't even here yet, and they were already putting a damper on her food and beverage options.

Smiling, Mackenzie replied, "Water is fine, thank you."

"Okay, I'll be right back," she said, closing the door behind her.

"Mrs. Vincent, please...have a seat," Mr. Graham advised. "How can I help you today?"

Mackenzie sat down, placing the envelope next to her. "I'm here to speak with you about filing for divorce. I need to get away from my husband as fast as possible, and I need to know all of my options," she stated frankly.

"Alright then," he nodded. "Straight to the point. Not a problem. Can you tell me about your situation?"

A knock at the door interrupted them and Mackenzie turned and saw his receptionist had returned with her water. Accepting it, Mackenzie thanked her, and she left again.

"Continue," he said.

Detail after detail, Mackenzie spent the next forty-five minutes telling him everything about her marriage to Jasper. Good and bad. The abuse. Her moderate involvement with his operation. Her pregnancy. She didn't leave out one piece of information. As much as she wanted to skimp on the details, particularly the parts where she was a complete fool, she knew if she wanted help, she had to bare her soul. Periodically, she'd see his facial expressions shift, but he remained silent as she unveiled all her secrets.

"I see," he finally said. "Well, Mrs. Vincent, I won't lie to you. You have quite a situation on your hands, but it's nothing I haven't dealt with before."

Mackenzie was relieved to hear it, seeing as though she'd done her homework regarding the best divorce attorneys in Atlanta. Mitchell Graham was number two on that list, meaning he was probably the right about of bulldog and viper she needed. The moment Jasper was served with papers, he would come for her with everything he could. Therefore, she needed to make sure she had someone ruthless on her side.

"However, I will tell you this because I believe in preparing my clients for the worse. If your soon-to-be ex-husband is anything like you've described—this won't be easy—and he won't let you go without a fight. It won't necessarily be because he wants to remain married to you versus he doesn't want to lose. You need to be ready for that."

"I understand," Mackenzie said.

"You also need to be prepared for this being drug out during the duration of your pregnancy, so I have to ask—are you sure you want to do this right now? I understand you have a domestic violence situation on your hands, but divorces can be exhausting and emotionally taxing. That's a lot to handle for a pregnant woman."

Normally, she'd take offense to his mansplaining pregnancy to her, but Mackenzie appreciated his concern and considered his advice on the strength he may have encountered in a situation like hers.

"I understand, but my safety and the safety of my child is my priority right now. And the longer I am legally tied to him, the higher the risk. He's already shown up at my mother's house twice and threatened her. I'm not going another eight months under duress and looking over my shoulder."

"If you're sure," he said, confirming her decision.

"What do you need from me, Mr. Graham?"

He grinned at her response. It was clear she was a fighter and not willing to back down; therefore, he'd stand in the gap for her. He pressed the button on his phone to summon his assistant.

"Alicia, can you bring me a blank file please? For divorce," he clarified.

"Yes sir," she replied and hung up. Seconds later, she was at his door with a manila folder that contained papers."

He waited for her to leave and then said, "Alright, so I'm going to run down the process of getting a divorce in Georgia. Since the chance of this being contested, I'll start with that first and then let you know how it'll go if it's uncontested."

Not likely, Mackenzie thought as he went over everything. She sat listening to him, mentally noting everything as he laid the process out from start to finish. In the back of her mind, she began to formulate her plan in the event he wanted to make this harder than it needed to be. She remembered her father's words, *"A bird in the hand is worth two in the bush,"* as she collected what she needed from the house.

Jasper was the type to push the limits, and she wanted to be ready just in case he'd cut his nose to spite his face. She knew his pressure points just like he knew hers. Compliments of his control issues and feeling the need to always keep her so close. Still, he was unpredictable and unhinged. She needed to be equally unpredictable.

"Do you have any questions for me?" he asked.

"None that I can think of. You've covered just about everything."

"Oh…wait…I forgot to tell you my rate," he remembered. "My hourly rate is four hundred dollars per hour."

Mackenzie didn't flinch. She figured he'd land somewhere between three and six hundred dollars thanks to a simple Google search since he was one of the best. Reaching into her purse,

Mackenzie retrieved the stack of money she set aside for this appointment. Placing it on the desk, she slid it toward him.

He looked down at the bills neatly stacked and wrapped in a currency strap labeled—ten thousand. Slowly, he lifted his head and gazed at her.

"That's enough to get started, correct?" she asked.

"More than enough. Let's get started."

EPILOGUE

Three weeks later

"Hey, you got pretty quiet over there," he said, glancing at her while they were stopped at the light. "Are you okay?"

"Just inside of my head," she admitted, staring out of the window.

"You want to talk about it?"

Alexis gazed at him. "Honestly, it's nothing."

"It's something. You went from talking to complete silence. Usually, when you do that, you're thinking hard."

"You don't know me like that, Dr. Harper," she teased.

He chuckled. "I know you better than you think I do. I haven't just been consumed with our physical interactions. I've paid attention to how you move around outside of the bedroom, so tell me…what's going on inside of that head of yours."

"All my life, I've never cared about people liking me or accepting me. Though now, I can't help that I want him to, but on the other hand, I don't care. If I'm being frank, I'm more upset than anything, and I'm doing my best to rally this need to go in there and rip him to shreds."

Keith pulled in front of the building and parked. Grabbing her hand, he held it.

That's understandable—your anger, the frustration—every single emotion you have stirring inside of you is okay for you to feel that way. If I were in your shoes, I'd feel the same way, but remember—you get more flies with honey than you do vinegar. You want answers, and the only way to get them is to keep a level head."

"You said that like I'm going to go in there and tear the place up."

Keith furrowed his brow. "Alexis Bayou. I've worked with you for at least two years now, and I've seen your good and your bad side, and I will be the first to admit—I want no parts of that bad side."

Alexis laughed.

He laughed too. "Exactly."

Alexis toyed with her fingers.

"Are you nervous?"

Alexis shrugged. "I'm not sure. I mean, a part of me is, but the other part of me is ready to know the truth. Guess I just didn't think I'd be going about it this way."

"You're doing what you have to do," he said, resting his free hand on top of hers, "Don't beat yourself up for that. It's an admirable quality, one that I admire about you. You're determined, and you don't take no for an answer when it's something you really want to know."

"I'm not; I just feel like all of this is so unnecessary. I hate that I feel like I'm the sneaky one now."

"I understand that, all things considered, but as I said, sometimes when you aren't given the answers, you have to seek them out yourself."

Alexis smiled and nodded as she lowered her head to read the information Chester had sent her again. She'd come all this way, so turning around seemed futile. Every mile they drove, her heart pounded against her chest. She came close to telling him to get off and turn around at just about every exit they passed, but she pressed forward. Even if nothing came from this, at least she knew.

"Thank you for coming with me, Keith. I appreciate it. Especially since you didn't have to spend your off weekend doing this."

Keith winked. "It's no trouble at all," he replied sincerely. "I told you I'm here for you, and at this point, I feel vested in your quest to learn about who you are. It's quite refreshing to be honest. Learning about you while you're learning about you."

Alexis smiled on the inside. His words moved Alexis. She couldn't believe he'd been this person all this time, and she'd looked past him, mostly, due to her own trust issues. While the rest was her simply not wanting to be involved with anyone, she worked with ever again. But Keith was relentless, determined like he said she was. He wholeheartedly believed they would be a great team, and she was beginning to see that. Though her heartbreak with Quinn left a pretty bad taste in her mouth, the more time she spent with Keith, she came to realize they were nothing alike.

He'd gone above and beyond what any man would do for someone they weren't romantically involved with. And for that reason alone, she owed it to herself…and him, to be open to the possibility of something more than sex.

"I just hope it doesn't blow up my face," Alexis uttered softly. "I'd hate for this to feel like a wasted trip."

"Nothing about this is wasted. If it turns out to be a bust, at least you were able to face this head-on. And later, we'll figure out how to move forward. But we won't know which option to pursue until you leave the car, and walk in there."

His encouragement was refreshing, Alexis thought to herself as she stared out of the window.

So was his optimism. As much as she wanted to get her hopes up, she was trying to remain calm. Hopeful but calm. She didn't want to get her hopes up since she'd hit a couple of brick walls, only adding to her frustration. She felt her aunt might know something, but she also knew there was a sister code they upheld, kind of like the one she had with hers. Miriam had always been sharp, quick-witted, and very smart. She sort of reminded her of Mackenzie in how she could think on her feet. She'd always been so agile in her thinking that even when they thought they'd gotten one past her, she'd be several steps ahead of them. That was Mackenzie in a nutshell.

"You're right. We've come this far," Alexis said, unbuckling her seatbelt.

"Did you want me to come inside with you?"

Alexis contemplated his offer, thinking it might be better if she did this on her own. If she needed him, she'd come to get him. Until then, she'd lace up her boots and stand tall. Leaning over, she gave him a soft peck on the lips.

"Thank you, but you've done enough. I need to take these next steps by myself. If I need you, I'll call you."

Keith nodded. "Okay, I can do that."

Alexis inhaled the deepest breath she could then exhaled.

"You got this champ," he cheered her on.

Pulling the handle, Alexis opened the door and got out. Each step she took toward the door felt like she was moving stacks of bricks. A fleet of emotions had been set off inside her, and she felt like she was a circus's ringmaster. Only the circus was her life. She opened the door and was greeted by a cool breeze and the smell of flowers. The inside was brightly lit due to the overhead lighting and natural light beaming in from the large windows. Behind the receptionist's desk was a live plant wall full of plants cascading down. Alexis grinned, concluding he was where she got her love of plants from.

The soft nature sounds flowed from the speakers. She was grateful for the relaxed setting and hoped things stayed that way. Alexis approached the desk with a friendly smile. The two ladies behind it returned the gesture.

"Hello," Alexis greeted them. "I'm here to see Dr. Alexander."

The older lady maintained her eye contact. "Hello and welcome. May I ask your name?"

Alexis hesitated. She wasn't sure how she wanted to introduce herself. She was torn between saying her first name or her last. Settling on her both, she responded, "Alexis Bayou."

Initially, she was going to go with *his daughter* but decided that was a bit too forward. She didn't want to come off like a crazy stalker. Especially if they knew him and had been working for him for some time, another piece of information she'd learned from Chester's findings was that he had a daughter, so that would definitely be awkward.

"Okay, if you would like to have a seat, I'll let him know you're here to see him."

Alexis nodded and turned to find a seat. Truthfully speaking, she'd rather stand. Her legs already felt wobbly. The last thing she wanted to do was be suddenly struck with paralysis when he walked out. Walking over to the window, she signaled to Keith with a thumbs up to let him know things were all good so far.

He mimicked her signal.

Spotting a water filter in the corner, Alexis walked over and filled a cup up. She gulped two cups down before tossing them in the trash. Her nerves were getting the best of her. She moved to sit down when the door opened, and Daniel appeared.

Alexis watched as the door closed behind him. Her eyes returned to him as he stood in his white coat with confusion flooding his face. Suddenly she questioned whether or not Grace had actually told him or if that was just a diversion, she deployed to keep from telling her the truth.

Fidgeting with her hands, Alexis stared into the eyes of the man who made up half of her DNA. She searched his face for some resemblance and found some. She'd always known she favored Grace but seeing him now—the resemblance was uncanny. Alexis kicked herself for not paying closer attention when he was at the repast. She was so wrapped up in her grief, Grace's random fainting, and the other guests—he'd gotten past her.

Alexis swallowed and then parted her lips. "Daniel…"

"Alexis…"

Dear Reader,

I hope you enjoyed my book.

Please make sure to leave a review on my author page on Amazon.

Thank you,

Tess Flowers

Make sure to pre-order Book 4, *Dreams and New Beginnings*, the final chapter in The Bayou Sisters' story. Coming September 2023.

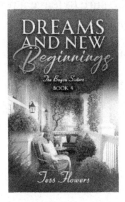

JOIN MY NEWSLETTER TO RECEIVE UPDATES ABOUT NEWS AND TO GET A FREE COPY OF "WHERE IT ALL BEGAN," PREQUEL OF CLOSELY GUARDED SECRETS.

www.authortessflowers.com/sample

Made in the USA
Monee, IL
03 August 2023

40410761R00214